Child of Dust

Mike Jenkins

Gomer

First Impression – 2005

ISBN 1 84323 491 2

This book is published with the financial support
of the Welsh Books Council.

*Printed in Wales at
Gomer Press, Llandysul, Ceredigion SA44 4JL*

*To the memory
of my great friend and comrade,
Jack Gilbert*

Acknowledgements

Some of these stories have appeared previously in a variety of publications, including *Graffiti Narratives* (Planet), *Magpies* (Gomer), *Mama's Baby (Papa's Maybe)* (Parthian), *Wales in Our Own Image* (In Books), *In Enemy Territory* (Edge Press), *Cambrensis*, *Anglo-Welsh Review*, *Planet*, *The Interpreter's House* and *New Welsh Review*.

Contents

	page
Who is the Stalker?	9
The Terrapin Factor	24
Allotment for Memories	48
Realising the Garden	53
Schuhmacher's Collapse	57
Changing the Script	66
In Enemy Territory	77
Dead Hero Silence	89
Avin a Field Day	97
The Davies Gang	109
Novelties	115
Lost Ighway	123
Some Kind o' Beginnin	130
Sara's Story	139
Cellohead	141
The Leader	142
Petrified Music	143
Crack	145
Child of Dust	146
Barry Island Lines	149
Promising Light	151
Above Us, The Deed	152
Partly Political Conference	154
Strange Fish	155
Letter to Engels	156
Girl on the Viaduct	159
Scott Guru	168
No Ordinary House	179
Houses are Marching	188
Barnardo's Boy	189
Duel in the Snow	190
Just Like Kerouac	191

Who Is the Stalker

Who is the Stalker?

I want to live forever. I don't care what anybody says. It was Flanders, supposedly a romantic holiday in Bruges. 'Revive your marriage!' is what my dear mother said. In Flanders, where my wife drove through land as distant from war graves as you could imagine, with industrial units lining a motorway of juggernauts. She was cursing their spray when I hit it (or it hit me). It was a wall of ice, a cold I'd never experienced before. I felt alone and envied her faith. The coldness went right to my core.

'You are going to die,' it insisted. 'One day you won't be here and the world will go on as if you'd been a fly zapped by spray. You will be nothing.'

I couldn't argue back. Man had invented heaven to explain the one thing totally beyond comprehension. Hell was an ideal way of asserting power. That moment in Flanders – where so many had been slaughtered – I shivered and could not stop the freezing thoughts which filled my veins. It paralysed me. I could talk about so many forbidden things, but not the D-word.

She focussed straight on, dead on. The map sat on my lap like a reluctant child I patted occasionally.

I knew I had to defeat it. It wouldn't go away. I remembered nothing about the time before I was born, but that had been shared, a communal place like a vast, cloudy waiting-room. I could see the temptations to create your own version: angels serving tortillas and guacamole, the best bitter straight from the barrel, with their feathers white as your age and a line of cirrus for every wrinkle.

Yet, there was always a doubt, sins counting against me. Something I shouldn't even believe in which still crept in.

We'd gone to Belgium to avoid the heat of the Med. What did we get but 35 degrees in the shade and unbearable night-time stickiness? A twin bed with a crevice down the middle that even Chris Bonnington would have problems crossing. The first night back home I awoke to piss out that delectable Trappist beer we'd brought back and couldn't get back to sleep. I sighed steeply for lack of sex and woke my wife from her snoring bliss.

'What's the matter?'

'Can't sleep.'

'I gathered that – just relax.'

'I'm going to die, Hannah!' There, I'd come out with it. To avoid telling the truth, initially, but it was vital just to utter those words.

'What? Is your stomach playing you up again?'

'No. I mean I'm definitely going to die. I can't stop thinking about it.'

'Have you got a date for it? Have you turned Red Indian? For goodness' sake Dave, stop going on. You practically spoiled our holiday with that bloody bed. You always need something to worry about. You won't have time when we're back at work.'

'I'm sorry. I just –'

She turned her back and went to sleep, as if she could switch it on and off. I can see what drives people to drink, where there's no tomorrow and no consequences. I can see how people lose their brain-cells when they get old, not just from disease but desire. It's too dark out there. For a species who can clone, we haven't a clue. Even if I became a spirit, who's to say I'd be summoned to appear? No! I want a 0.3333-recurring guarantee.

I've even contemplated visiting my wife's church and going to confession.

'Yes, my son. What mortal sins have you committed?'

'I'm absolutely terrified of dying, Father.'

'Well, as long as you've been a good Christian, you'll go to heaven.'

'I have no faith, Father. I need a ticket, preferably a return, just to get a glimpse of the place. I'd like to accompany my wife. You see, our holiday . . .'

Or a travel agent's, would they oblige? Neil Roberts, who used to work in our office, works in one down town. I could try him.

'Neil, can you do me a cheap flight to Hades?'

'Hades? Let me see, is that one of the Greek islands?'

'Close in terms of temperature. No, it's supposed to be hell.'

'So why go there?'

'Just to experience it.'

'Dave, you always were off it.'

'Will I burn there, Neil? Will sun-block work where no parasols or trees give shade?'

11

After Belgium, the moles appeared, my skin a pocked lawn. One, in particular, was inflamed, itched and bled. I began to avoid the sun like she avoided sex. A mere touch of its rays and I'd scurry for cover. I'd examine streets for shade, like a lizard after camouflage.

My wife wanted children desperately, though how exactly we were going to achieve this without intercourse didn't seem to enter the equation. We'd been tested and neither of us seemed to have any defect, but I got the blame. My sperm were as bloody-minded as me. As she constantly spurned me, I became convinced she was seeing someone. I even followed her to church, but our car was parked outside. Halfway home it occurred to me that either she met him there or he lived nearby! Sniffing around her when she returned, she got very uppity.

'Are you turning into a bloodhound, David Hopkins?'

'New perfume?'

'Shut up!'

'Incense in church?'

'Give over, will you? You're driving me crazy!'

I went to the doctor's with my irritable mole. In the waiting room I did feel it was trivial, even though I was convinced it was cancerous. The female doctor told me inflamed moles were common, especially with middle-aged men. I was just about to announce that I was dying, when she dismissed me politely.

I vowed to tell Hannah that I'd to go for more tests, and that it was serious. Maybe pity would open her to me?

12

As I walked back to the car in the fading light, I could make out someone in the distance. He had his back to me and was tampering with the bonnet. I yelled out, 'Hey! What are you doing?' He ran off without turning and I had a curious feeling that he was wearing an old coat of mine, a green frayed one I'd used in the garden.

By the time I got home I'd convinced myself the man was Hannah's lover, that she'd given him my coat and he was investigating the car in order to kill me.

But the coat was there on its peg and by the time she came home from the office, I knew I'd make her feel guilty.

'How did the doctor's go, Dave?'

I toyed with my chips – instead of the usual hearty construction of a chip butty and crack-jaw gobbling.

'It doesn't look great. I've got to go for further tests.'

'When?'

'Don't know. The hospital will contact me.'

'I'm sure you'll be okay, Dave.'

'I knew we should have taken out life insurance – just in case.'

'Don't be so silly – mind, you have got a point!'

'What?'

I glared incredulously. Pushed aside my plate. Left the table, moping and hurt. Lay on the bed, curled up. She joined me – after the news – and stood over me, impatient.

'Why don't you lie down, Hannah?'

'Dave!'

13

'Come on, why not? We used –'

'One moment you're dying, the next you want sex! I give up!'

We didn't speak the rest of the evening. Going to bed I stared down our quiet street. Blocking the narrow alley at the end of the Close was a figure, under a street-light. He was about my size and as I strained to make him out, he appeared to lift an arm in acknowledgement. Hannah lay in bed, hunched and self-contained as ever.

'There's a weird bloke standing over there. I'm sure it's the same one I saw messing with our car earlier. Come and see if you recognise him.'

'What? – Dave, you woke me up! Just get into bed and shut up, will you?'

A look back and he'd gone. Probably strolled off down the alley.

I pestered Hannah and eventually she gave in, more to get some sleep than out of genuine interest. She kissed the worst mole and it stung, but I didn't react.

By morning it had almost vanished. It was flat, boring and didn't look a threat. When she noticed I claimed it was a miracle.

'You see, sex is good for my moles. Several times a week and they'll be cured completely.'

'God, Dave, you've turned into a bloody hypo!'

'Yeah, I made up the bleeding and itching.'

'Well, you won't have to go to hospital.'

'No I won't, 'cause I made that up as well!'

Her brown eyes squinted as they always did when she was unsure.

Later that week she dyed her hair with a yellowy tinge and I got really worried. As often happened when I was in a quandary, events took over. My present post had arrived like that, a chance encounter with the man (now my boss) at a struggling computer firm I used to work for.

I left work early to meet Hannah. I don't know why, but I did have it in mind to make it up to her, if only to destroy her 'barrier method'! As I parked close to the plush new office of accountants and solicitors where she worked, I spied him quite clearly. This time it was his back, leaving the building and heading for the County Hall. Just as before, he wore that old coat, only with the hood up. He was hunched and awkward, a gait which resembled my own.

I wanted to scream out so that he turned, but instead all my anger sped me to Hannah's office. She was sitting at her desk, calmly talking on the phone, preoccupied till I stood in front of her, hands raised in exasperation. She made an excuse and put down the receiver.

'Dave! What the hell's the matter? Why aren't you at work? Have you been –'

'He's been here, hasn't he?'

'Who?'

'The bloke. Him! The man I saw. The bloke from the alley!' I spat.

'Dave, keep your voice down! For Chrissake, what are you on about?'

'I saw him outside. Who the fuckin' hell is he, Hannah?'

15

'Look! Just stop shouting, will you?'

At that point one of her senior partners, Richard, came in, attracted by the commotion.

'Everything okay, Hannah? Oh, it's you, Mr Hopkins. I thought it was some rowdy divorcee or something. I'll leave you to it.'

'Not far wrong, Richard,' she muttered as he left the room.

'Who is he, Hannah? I want to know. You've got to come clean!'

She laughed mockingly. I felt small as a scolded child.

'Look, Dave, I don't know and I don't care. I just wish you'd stop being so bloody paranoid. I can't take much more of it.'

I gazed deep into her. She seemed so credible.

'It's a strange coincidence, that's all. He keeps cropping up.'

'Maybe he's a stalker.'

'What, after you?'

'No, he could be stalking you. After all, you were in the surgery; and then he has got a thing about your coat.'

'The coat. Yeah, you're right.'

And with a curt goodbye I rushed home. If she'd stolen it to give to him, I'd soon find out. But it was there on the peg as usual, looking unrufffled. I hauled it outside and flung it onto the garden path. I put a match to it and watched it burn, as if I was guilty of a crime and was destroying the evidence. Onlooking neighbours would be suspicious.

When Hannah returned she soon noticed the coat had gone, its distinctive blue cheese whiff missing.

'What did you do with it, Dave? Eat it on crackers or something?'

'What?'

'That old coat!'

'Why should you notice it?'

'Just because –'

'I set fire to it!'

'What's the point of that? It was a museum piece. You're definitely mad!'

I walked off in disgust, thinking of what she'd previously said. Stalking me? It didn't make sense; was she trying to put me off the trail? I had a mission to finish. I had to track him down and confront him.

Lunchtimes – normally sacrosanct – were devoted to his pursuit. I parked my car at various locations, then walked to a vantage point. There I'd look back and wait to see if he'd tamper with it or snoop. But there was no sight of him. Sometimes I just wandered around the shops, stopping in doorways and peering back to see if he was shadowing me. I relished this detective work, though it was fruitless. Then my boss asked to see me urgently. He was gentle but threatening.

'Dave, you know I'm a tolerant man, but this is going over the top.'

'What is, Gwyn?'

'This lunchtime business. Every lunch hour you're out and you come back late. If you're meeting someone, for God's sake do it out of business hours. You're costing us!'

'I'm sorry, honest. I didn't realise.'

'Just get it sorted, will you?'

'Okay, definite. By the way, Gwyn, how are the boys? Not causing you any distress, I hope.'

'Just worry about yourself. All right?'

He knew I had him. His sons had been arrested for criminal damage, but when arrested he'd pulled ropes rather than strings. I couldn't push him too far, but neither could he risk being exposed. Moreover, what else did our firm produce but roller-blinds for shops? And his two little darlings were actually found smashing the windows of several businesses who hadn't purchased our products. An odd coincidence.

I decided to restrict my investigations to twice a week, preferably when Gwyn was out visiting clients.

Before going to bed I still checked the street. I stood with binoculars fixed on the alleyway, when Hannah came upstairs.

'Dave, what are you looking for? A full moon?'

'Hannah, just give over. He could come any time.'

'Which is more than I'm likely to do. Well, at least it's stopped you going on about death all the time.'

'No', I thought, 'this is a much more vital obsession.'

On an impulse, the next day I again parked round the corner from her office, this time during lunch. Several people exited, including Hannah herself, which was strange as she always claimed she had a working lunch. I dipped down in case she turned, afterwards realising she'd have recognised our car anyway.

Suddenly, he came out. No green coat, of course, but a creamy jacket that was unmistakably mine. I saw him from behind, the slouching walk singling him out. I rushed from the car, sprinted up to him, grabbing and twisting him round forcefully. I began to punch and swear. He shoved me away and I was aghast. The jacket was nothing like mine and he resembled someone from Hannah's work. His jittering eyes spelled recognition.

'Er – sorry – I'm mistaken!' I stuttered, retreating to my car, pale and shaking.

'Hey, come back! What the hell's going on?' I could hear him yelling as I drove off.

That evening I knew Hannah would interrogate me.

'My God, Dave, what have you done now? Mr Symons, one of the accountants, you practically strangled him! You could get done for assault. It was caught on the closed circuit. Are you deliberately trying to humiliate me? Do you want me to lose my job, or what?'

'I'm really sorry, Hannah. I thought it was him.'

'So who's stalking who? Now you seem to be the bloody stalker, don't you?'

I sulked upstairs, out of the way, and scanned the street again, hoping to prove her wrong. A figure came down the alley, but it was only Jim Davies from up the street, trying desperately to sober up before he got home.

The phone rang and she answered. I could hear

19

her murmuring and crept onto the landing, ear low like a child to a railway line.

'Dave! It's your mother, she wants a word.' Her tone was ominous. I hurried downstairs.

'Yes, mum, what is it?'

'David, I'm most concerned. Hannah tells me you've been behaving very strangely. Don't you think you should get professional advice?'

'You mean a shrink? Okay, what's she been saying?'

'You accosted one of her colleagues, David. It's not like you. It would be for your own good. Maybe you've been working too hard –'

'Just leave us alone, mum. I'll sort it out, honest. You're right, it's the pressure of work. I promise I'll visit soon. Now please don't fret. 'Bye.'

I put the phone down before she could broach her usual question. It was more than I could face at that moment. Hannah came from the kitchen, smugness drawn across her features.

'Why tell her? Why involve her, when she's got enough to worry about with dad's illness?'

'Maybe you'll listen to her, that's why. You just ignore me.'

I stood over her with knife-point eyes. She didn't flinch, laughing at me without making a sound.

'You think I'm a bloody nutter. Well, we'll see!'

I returned to my look-out post. It was a clear night, the full moon at its height. If she wanted to dub me a lunatic, then the time was ripe. Our street was deserted and quiet as downtown Sunday. I could hear her guffawing at Victoria Wood on telly. So close together, yet so many miles away. I shifted focus to the top of a slight hill in our Close and spotted a man leaning against a garden wall. There was no street-light where he stood, so I couldn't make him out exactly. It could be someone waiting for a friend or walking the dog, of course, but he seemed to be aping my stare. He moved downhill a little way and it was as if moonlight caught him. The coat resembled the one I'd burned the other day. It couldn't be!

No rushing. Cool and calculated this time. Passing Hannah with, 'Going for a quick walk. See you.' Sharp kitchen knife slid into my pocket. Kidnap him, evidence at last.

But as soon as I unlatched our gate, he put up his hood and began to stride away. All my intended calm disappeared. Seeing my prey go round the corner, I ran in a frenzy. Up the street, round the bend, heart triggering my loathing. He started to run too and I flung myself at him, dragging him round to face –

I pushed him away instantly with revulsion. My own features mocked back at me, grinning. A nightmare? Madness? He was real enough, I could feel.

Instinctively, I drew out the knife. He spoke. I spoke.

'What good will it do to harm me? You'll only be hurting yourself.'

'Who are you? I've got no twin. My mother never –'

I held up the blade so it almost touched his cheek, defying the mask to slip.

'Do you know everything?' He sneered, and seemed to read every thought as if it were print.

'Why have you been following me? What do you want?'

21

I kept the knife high, but he showed no fear.

'Me following you? That's a laugh! Anyway, I've got something you need. We could do a deal.'

'How do you mean. You blackmailing me? Is this something my mum shouldn't know about?'

'No, it's here.' He touched his trouser zip. 'Do you want me to show you?'

'What are you trying to say, you bastard?' I lunged the knife at him, but he dodged out of the way, chuckling and pointing accusingly.

'You want children; I can give you them. Well, not you, but your wife. Tell you what, I'll give you this coat back and for that I get to screw her till she gets pregnant. How's that?'

'What? Don't be so fuckin' stupid. You're crazy!'

'No, you're the one who's mad not to accept. You can return to your wife after and she won't know any difference.'

At that moment I could have murdered him – this impostor, wearing my face as though he owned it.

'Let me go with her and you won't see me again. Your face will be your own. If you refuse I'll be back. I won't let you go.'

A stray dog came along the street, sniffed at his trousers and was about to cock a leg when he kicked it. I knew I had to live with his presence, in the same way I had to come to terms with death. I gave him a hefty shove and he staggered. He righted himself and hurried off, muttering, 'I won't give up!'

He left so many questions, I couldn't disentangle them. My head buzzed. A twin? Adoption? Had I hallucinated? Did she spike my tea with tablets to induce madness? Did he think I'd agree to his plan? But kids – wouldn't that solve so much? I even felt a sense of regret. Perhaps I should have got to know him?

Back to the childless house. No toys, no photos, no cuttings of success.

His face had been hollower than mine, his eyes sunken and skin more stretched. He was paler, yet claimed something I'd never possess.

Back in our lounge, Hannah stood at the window. There was a gap in the curtains. The lights were off.

'What were you up to, Dave?'

'I told you, I went for a short walk.'

'Short walk? You were haring up the close like a maniac and what's that knife doing in your hand?'

I gazed down at the kitchen knife I still clutched.

'It's all right, there's no blood on it!'

'Oh, that's a relief. So you haven't actually killed anybody then? Just practising, is it? Honestly, Dave, I give up!'

She sank into an armchair. She'd made a decision. I could read that in her eyes. If only she knew the sacrifice I'd made. After all, I had to live with that man. The stalker, whoever he was.

I sat opposite her, but she avoided my glances. It was a warm night, but I felt that same icy wave rush into me and remain. One day you will be nothing, was its refrain.

The Terrapin Factor

Nothing was working out for the Council. The Millennium celebrations had been a total disaster. The bonfires had all been lit at 4.30 in the afternoon to avoid trouble from marauding gangs – and nobody had noticed them at all. The play put on by a local youth theatre lauding the famous writer Nicholas Jones was due to be staged the week after a TV documentary exposed him as a closet fascist. The attendance was so poor even the complimentary VIP tickets weren't taken. Worst of all was a Schools Swimming Gala. This was organised by a lifeguard whose brother was married to the Mayor's sister.

The idea he had was an all-schools extravaganza in Giant's Bite pool down the valley. He invited every Junior school there. It caused traffic chaos right down to Fiddler's Elbow, a notorious bend in the road. Thousands of pupils, parents and teachers descended on the swimming pool, which was the size of a large classroom and had no spectator seating. As parents shoved to the water's edge there were fears for their safety. The fire brigade and police were called and the pool evacuated before a single race was swum. Irate parents turned on teachers as the organizer crept out of the back door. The Great Millennium Swim was never to be repeated.

The Chief Executive Richard Moffatt, known as 'Dick' (or worse, to his enemies), was busy taking the flak for these catastrophies. He needed to come up with a solution rapidly and the obvious choice was someone dependable, who could also deliver.

There was only one person in the Civic Centre who fitted the bill perfectly. He was a staid, conformist yes-man. He was a member of the Labour Party and a Male Voice choir, and lived in Cwmtaff but spoke like a newsreader. He had a charming wife and daughter and no opinions to speak of. He was Morgan Howells, known affectionately as 'Morg'. He was totally reliable. After all, he'd even helped organize the dinner for the new mayor paid for by Celtic Power who were due to carry out opencast mining near Morgan's own house. The property value would drop from £100,000 to £40,000 if planning permission were granted, but he still took the money and ensured personally that the vol-au-vents were crisp.

Morg was Head of Personnel and thus an expert at choosing the right person for a job. Anyone with opinions or face-rings was discounted immediately.

When he was summoned to Moffatt's office, he thought he'd done something wrong. He thought it was about the recently-appointed young man in Housing who'd proved erratic and argumentative, saying the tenants should be informed about the details of private buy-outs of their estates, instead of being bribed to agree to them by promises of money for repairs.

'The truth! The cheek of it! His truth more like it!'

Morg worried, as he went up in the lift to Moffat's HQ.

Richard Moffatt had a large map of the town stretched across the floor of his office. It was like a large Monopoly board, except that on it were mouse-sized black and white counters, strategically placed. The Chief leapt out of his seat on seeing Morgan, his head as polished as his desk. Morg slipped on a black counter as he approached, and bent down to try to replace it in the correct position.

'The Millennium Duck Race, Mr Howells. Organized at a time of drought!'

'What do the white ones represent, Mr Moffatt?' They'd known each other for years, but remained very formal.

'Developments, Mr Howells, developments. New roads leading to sites not yet built. Proposals for shopping complexes which could yet end up as car-parks. There's a great deal happening in this town. Above all, three prominent white discs to signify opencast mining schemes. As you know . . . Celtic Power . . . but enough of this . . .'

Moffatt sat-stood on the edge of his desk. Morgan was perched uncomfortably on the rim of the map, feeling like a lowly captain in the General's presence.

'That Evans fellow in Housing, I can explain . . .'

'Who? Oh, it doesn't matter. He's practically gone anyway. No, a much more serious issue to be raised.'

By now Morg's bladder was a pin-cushion. Was he too old at forty and being told to consider re-training. 'There's a nice part-time job in the Library Service' sprang to mind.

'Frankly, David in Leisure hasn't delivered. What about you organizing a one-off? David will agree to it. I went on holiday with him a couple of years ago and I know a certain club in Amsterdam where he let himself go, shall we say. What do you say, Morgan . . . you're The Man!'

All of a sudden, Moffatt had skirted round the map and was within handshake distance, all beams.

'A one-off?'

'Listen. There's a fair bit of Millennium cash left. We've blown it so far. We need a success. No pressure mind. You'll think of something, I'm sure. Nothing extravagant, of course. Just something that bloody well works. Agreed?'

Moffatt was shaking his hand vigorously before he had the chance to consider. He was chuffed though. What had he done to be so honoured?

'Naturally, the money has got to be spent this year. How about New Year's Eve?'

'Wasn't that last year?'

'No, we can make it a gimmick, surely. Celebrate the Millennium a year late. We've got to do something, or we'll look stupid. I'll fax you a breakdown of the budget. Agreed?'

'Er . . . well . . .'

'Thought you would!'

On his way home to 'Magmorg', 69 Castle View, he stopped in at the pet shop in town. It was cleverly called *Piranha Pop-In,* though Morg had never seen one for sale there. If he had he might've bought it, because tropical fish was his hobby. It had been since he was a boy and his dad had won a goldfish in Barry Island. Morg had been fascinated by its ability to swim round and round without any signs of boredom or frustration. Having a short memory was an unusual talent.

He possessed an attaché case with a special water-tight compartment built in. It was his only concession to eccentricity. He chose a terrapin because it had a face like his friend Ray Biffen. Or alternatively, it occurred to Morg that he may have chosen Ray as his friend because he resembled a terrapin. He was very pleased with it and christened it Milly (short for Millennium) to comemmorate his new assignment. Calling it 'Dom' after the Dome would be to tempt fate.

He'd met Ray at a Celtic Power function. Ray was manager of the local waste-disposal site and had been responsible for a number of improvements in the surrounding area. He was now greatly in favour of wind turbines on the ridge overlooking the landfill site. He joked that at least they'd blow all the litter away from the housing. He'd winked at Morg's wife Margaret after his quip. Ray dubbed Morg and his wife 'M & M Enterprises' from some novel he'd read.

Marg was cooking when he got home. She'd taken to making very elaborate meals recently, due to the preponderance of culinary programmes on TV. She'd become obsessed by presentation and garnishes. Usually, this meant they were fridge-cold by the time they reached the table and Morg had to send for a takeaway later in the evening, much to his wife's chagrin. Once the garnish had obscured the entire dish and he'd eaten it by mistake. Mint sprinkled in icing sugar proved to be particularly indigestible!

'I've got it!' he announced.

'I know love,' she pecked him routinely on the right cheek, 'there's a lot about. I thought Liz wuz comin down with summin las week, 'er nose looked awful red!'

'No, look!' he proudly displayed his terrapin. 'I've named her Millie after Millennium. Have a guess why?'

'Yew've got tickets t' the Dome? Or maybe that Big Wheel, the London Igh? Or even the new bridge what keeps wobblin?'

'No dear. I've got a very special mission at work. They've put me in charge of the Grand Cwmtaff Millennium Event! Me? . . . I can't think why, but I'm going to make the most of it.'

'Tha's great love,' she said and carried on chopping some green stuff. It had cost him a minor fortune in equipment and produce. Things he never even knew existed: blitzers and whizzers. Things that sounded like fireworks.

'Make shewer they pay yew proper.'

'Why, do you want to buy some new-fangled device?'

'Well, actually, a juicer . . .'

'Millie and I are going to celebrate. I'm looking forward to supper. What is it?'

'Fish! I could ewse that terrapin f' decoratio . . .'

'One of your little jokes, I hope?'

Morg skilfully transferred Millie into his large

fish-tank. The guppies and angelfish scattered as Millie finned arrogantly amongst them. Millie flipped and belly-flopped, taking over the tank at once.

'Millie! I need ideas. Whatever am I going to come up with?'

His daughter Liz turned up late for supper, missing the first course, melon balls in a soupy substance. Morg carefully spooned out the balls, avoiding the red gloop. Liz looked different. Her hair was tangled into strands. She sat down with a thump, ready for battle.

'Liz! What happened to your hair?'

It had also changed colour to bright orange rather than the usual white streaks.

'Yew could always get a job as a warning signal!' his wife witted.

'It's no' funny mam, it's a statement !'

'You should be thinking more about your bank statement, not looking ridiculous. And what about those twisty things?'

'Theyr dreadlocks, dad! I might be turnin Rasta. They smoke ganga as part o' theyr religion, y'know. Its cool.'

'Margaret. Translate!'

'It's like tha Bob What's-is-face. Yew know, died years ago. Tha reggae mewsic.'

'Rather old-fashioned for you, Liz.'

'Oo cares. I'll make up my own fashions . . . Anyway, wha's all this about opencast I yeard? Yew lot goin t' dig up the Common an ruin ev'rythin, is it?'

'Opencast mining creates jobs. That land is derelict,' Morg replied automatically.

'Foxes, buzzards, woodpeckers, larks . . . oh, yeah, there's even ponds out there with newts an loadsa frogs. Some fish lover yew are! . . . I s'pose theyr all derelict animals, eh? No need for 'em, 'cept when they unt foxes o' course!'

'Tha's enough o' politics. I'm fed up of it, spoilin ev'ry mealtime . . . What d' yew think o' the fish?'

'I haven't found any yet!' Morg poked at his plate dubiously.

'Don' be silly, yew've eaten it!'

'Oh sorry, thought that was artichokes or something.'

'Anyway, it's all locally grown produce. I didn go far f'r the fish.'

Liz glanced slyly over at Morg's prized tank, 'Which one, mam?'

Morg was horrified, then returned their laughter with a Santa parody of 'Ho, ho, ho!'

'What's Delia doin t'night, mam? I ope it's beans on toast. I carn take no more of this.'

'Don be s' cheeky Liz!'

Liz pointed her knife at him.

'Lissen, dad. I might become 'n eco warrior.'

'Good idea, Lizzy. There are plenty of mine-shafts out the Common. You and your weird friends could disappear down one.'

Later that evening, with Liz out of the way drinking, Morg asked his wife for advice on the scheme. He'd racked his brains for something popular which would also create a stir. Massed Male Voice choirs marching through town? Something to do with history perhaps, with a reconstruction of the well-known Cwmtaff Rising of 1833, including soldiers firing blanks and a mock-up building set on fire? It seemed impractical. The choirs, in particular, wouldn't agree to the walking bit.

'So what are we famous for, Margaret?'

'Violence?'

'Don't be silly . . .'

'There's boxin . . . same thing really.'

'I have to come up with something original that works . . . You aren't helping!'

'Sorr-ee . . . Bras! We've always made 'em, far as I cun 'member.'

'Boxing, bras . . . anything not beginning with "b"?'

'Yes, there's Oovers, in there?'

'Mmm . . . you may have something there . . . I'll give it a thought.'

A giant vacuum-cleaner to suck in all the criminals on Pen-y-bryn estate? Morg surprised himself with his imagination. Millie had definitely inspired him, but he couldn't marry the terrapin with the machine. A vacuum-cleaner race down the valley sounded too much like a charity stunt.

As Margaret watched her favourite repeat of 'Men Behaving Badly', he returned to his fish-tank for a solution.

Millie seemed to have expanded in a matter of hours. It was obviously an optical illusion. The terrapin was very frisky and pursued Morg's treasured angelfish in and out of the dangling plants. Just as 'vacuum' kept nagging his brain, he watched as Millie's mouth acted like a hoover-hose, drawing Mandy the angelfish in and swallowing her whole. Morg's mouth dropped open, like a dead cod on the slab.

'What! The murderer! Marg! Marg! . . . Come and look at this! It's appalling! She's eaten my prize angelfish!'

His wife mumbled a reply, so he went over and gesticulated, making sucking noises. She giggled and wriggled at Tony's guitar playing, as he explained the homicide.

'Maybe it's some sorta sign.'

'Only women could be so dozy,' he thought.

'Sign? . . . Yes, it's a sign that I should get rid of Milly straight away.'

'She's problee jest ungree. Put some more feed in-a tank. Yew'll see.'

Morg fed the fish and saw Milly gobble it up, the others only getting specks. He sat in the corner, sulking behind the local paper, the *Cwmtaff Gazette*, known as 'the Gas' at work. He contemplated ringing Ray Biffen, but Biffen lived in Brecon, loathed Cwmtaff ('Too many smelly people!' he joked, half-seriously. He could imagine Liz's reply – 'Nothin t' do with yewer lan'-fill site, I s'pose?').

He kept picturing Milly the ravenous creature, with its suction mouth. Totally uncharacteristically, the vision of a huge vacuum-cleaner the shape of a terrapin came to Morg. He wondered if Liz had slipped some of that LSD into his red wine. It was completely absurd, but he liked it. The Cwmtaff Tropical Fish Society would make him chairman.

33

Then, coincidentally, a photo drew his attention to the paper. It was of an actress wearing a very flimsy, almost non-existent dress. The designer was none other than Cwmtaff born-and-bred Damien King. Absolutely amazing! He was convinced that King had been a contemporary of Liz at Castle Comp. He avidly read the article like his terrapin scoffing the feed.

'That's it!' he announced to his wife, who was startled by this unusual passion, but not enough to take her eyes from Tony's inevitable wooing of Debs.

'Wha is?'

'I've got it!'

'I thought yew wuz comin down with summin. Shull I get yew some aspirin, or wha?'

'No, no – the Millennium event of course! It must be a homage to the good old Hoover and also a fashion show. Old and new Cwmtaff combined. The best of our traditions and the . . . what would Liz say . . . coolest of the cool?'

Now, at last, Marg was staring hard at her excitable husband, looking for signs of delirium. This was not her staid Morgan Howells, but some form of HyperMorg, a man possessed.

'Ave a word with Liz,' she said.

The next day he managed to corner Liz before she left for her mundane job in a local insurance office.

'Liz!'

'Dad, don' wanna know about it!'

'But I haven't even told you yet.'

'Mam explained . . . some kind of Millennium

34

event . . . Try a massive bonfire up yewr friend Biffen's tip, that ud be andy.'

She was avoiding him and heading for the kitchen. He blocked her way.

'Liz! You'll be interested. I want a fashion show . . . You knew that Damien King, didn't you? He's world-famous now apparently. I really want to show the positive side of Cwmtaff.'

'Mam said summin about Oovers . . . anyway, ee's a prat!'

'A prat?'

'Yeah, ee gets is models t' dress in dead animals.'

'What? Sheep corpses, you mean?'

'Well, furs anyway.'

'But he's cool, isn't he.'

'Yew do wha yew wan, why ask me?'

She skirted past him.

Later, at work he couldn't concentrate on reading job applications for the new casual, temporary clerical assistants they were appointing in every department on a lower wage scale than those who had to take early retirement owing to pressure of work. He took to doodling on his note-pad: on one side of the page a scantily-clad female body and on the other a giant terrapin with a phallic protruding tube.

Without a knock Moffatt entered, like Morg's conscience, and caught him at what seemed aimless scribbling. Morgan tried to shield his work, but Moffatt was a prying boss.

'What's this, Howells? Naughty pictures? Shouldn't you be coming up with something, eh?'

Morg scrumpled up the paper, thus adding to his guilt and embarrassment.

'That's it, Mr Moffatt . . . I mean, those are my ideas.'

'Mr Howells, I chose you for your famous reliability. Don't let me down now, will you?'

'No . . . er . . . let me explain . . . You see, I thought we could celebrate the vacuum-cleaner, and also fashion.'

'Fashion in Cwmtaff? You must be kidding. The only fashion round here is for one ear – after the other's been bitten off in some pub brawl. Vacuum-cleaners I like however. But I doubt if it would bring in the media. Anyway, here's your budget . . .' He handed Morgan the paperwork. 'We can only afford one event and it must be on New Year's Eve, remember.'

'Yes, Mr Moffatt. Thanks! I'll apply myself.'

'You'd better had.' He peered in the direction of the scrumpled paper ball.

Morg couldn't shake off his notion. Luscious females and a giant terrapin: it reminded him of a dream he'd once had. For a man who'd only ever written stories at school about what he'd done during the holidays, and his collection of jungle animal cards, Morg was drunk on his inspiration.

A single event? Of course, he'd combine the two. A forceful suction effect from that vacuum-cleaner would gently stir all those lacy materials. He was just a little too young to be a contemporary of Marilyn Monroe's uplifting skirt, but that was the memorable moment he hoped to achieve.

He was elated and decided to celebrate with a cappuchino and cake in the canteen. On the way he bumped into Ray Biffen accompanied by Frank Thomas, a powerful councillor who also owned a nearby chemical plant. Ray with his landfill and Frank with his toxic waste, the two went together like Cwmtaff and drunkenness.

Ray was too busy to chat, but promised to join Morg for lunch at their favourite watering-hole, The Newt. Meanwhile, Morg began to brood about his daughter Liz. Why couldn't she be like Damien King, instead of steadily declining into New Age travellerism, without the inclination to move around? He'd even offered her a decent post as a clerical worker, but she'd accused him of nepotism. Well, her exact words were 'yew're all up each other's arses.' Very refined for a graduate.

When he met Ray he was full of his deal and hardly paid attention to Morg's attempts at explaining his great idea.

'Thomas! . . . What a man! . . . He's got the rest of those councillors like that . . .' He placed his fist on a beer-mat.

Ray went to buy the beer and order baps. He was a CAMRA member and a real-ale bore. Whenever he started talking percents and hops, Morg would retaliate with tropical fish.

'Witches Brew!' He returned with two heavily hoppy-looking pints.

'Sorry, Ray?'

'The guest ale . . . Witches Brew. 5.2%, Crapston's

Brewery, Derbyshire. The real stuff. I can't believe these people drinking bottled dog-piss here.'

'I've bought a terrapin.'

'Oh yeah . . . What's it like?'

'It's like a little tortoise with fins.'

'No, I mean the beer?'

'A bit warm.'

'It's supposed to be. That's the correct drinking temperature.'

'Not for June! Anyway, the terrapin ate my angelfish. I couldn't believe it!'

'It did?' Ray actually sounded interested for once. 'Ate it, eh?'

He was lost in thought for a while. Morg explained all about his scheme. Biffen was disappointed there was no role for his firm in it, but livened up when he heard the size of the vacu-terrapin.

'Yes, I see . . . and think of all that dust. It would have to go somewhere . . .'

'It'll only be used on the day, I'd say.'

'Never mind, I'm diversifying.'

'Into what?'

'Can't say at the moment. You'll soon find out.'

Morg knew better than to pursue it. Getting secrets out of Ray Biffen was like getting a smile from Councillor Thomas, not rare but impossible.

On arriving home, the smell of spices greeted him. Margaret tasted of chilli. Still, it made a change from garlic.

'I like yew better since yew bought tha terrapin,' she insisted.

But when he went to clean out the tank and feed his beloved pets, he noticed another absence. Millie was lodged, motionless for once, on the pebbles. He knew something was missing and went through a mental roll-call.

Boris the Tiger Barb.
Bill the Bleeding-heart Tetra.
Gorby the Guppy.
Tony the Clown Loach.
Mo the Koi.

Where was little Gordon, the Gouromi? Absolutely no hint of him. He stirred the water. Maybe he'd hidden in one of the rock caverns? He poked about inside, the plastic scraper scaring the fish, but making no impact on a bloated Millie. Little Gordon was nowhere to be found. He recalled what he'd witnessed the day before.

'Assassin! Bloody brutal murderer!' he yelled, wielding the scraper like a sword.

'I take that back!' his wife called from the kitchen.

'She's done it again, Marg! I'm sure that terrapin's killed little Gordon!'

His wife served up another feast of delicacies at suppertime, but Morg was too preoccupied to really appreciate them. The starters were decidedly chewy.

'What's this then?'

'Ish quid,' Marg replied, her mouth full.

'Ee didn ask ow much!' Liz wittily interjected. 'Sick squid, more like.'

Margaret nearly choked laughing.

'We seem to have had fish a lot lately.'

'Thought yew liked fish, dad.'

Morgan wanted to announce that his scheme had been approved and that Hoover were willing to construct a giant terrapin in time for December 31st, 2000. He wanted to enthuse about his phone conversation with King's agent with a view to booking him and choice models. He wanted to, but he'd become very paranoic about his disappearing fish. He began to suspect his wife, not Millie.

'I don't honestly know if it's you or that bloody terrapin!' he blurted, transferring the contents of his mouth into a paper napkin.' Where can you buy squid in Cwmtaff, for goodness' sake?'

His wife glared at him, as if he were the murderer. His daughter just sighed, 'Oh my God!'

'Don' be s' silly, Morg. I wen up to Brecon an bought it. Yewr little Gordon wouldn be enough f' one portion ne' mind three! Though I did think about Gorby as the main course.'

Liz did horse impersonations with her lips. He was sorry now he'd been so foolish. The two women seized their moment of strength.

'I need the Rover tomorrow t' go t' Cardiff,' said Marg.

'An I need the Panda t' go t' Bristol f'ra demo,' Liz added.

'To Bristol for a demo? Why can't they have demos in Cwmtaff . . . Second thoughts, you're better off over there. Just don't get arrested, that's all.'

'I'll give yew a list of frewt an veg t' get in the market,' his wife commanded.

At his time of power and triumph, Morg still felt like a subject in his own home.

Morg was perplexed by the sheer difficulty of shopping in Cwmtaff. When he enquired about a kumquat at the greengrocer's he was greeted with a derisory grin.

'I don' know the Welsh names f'r any of ower frewt,' the assistant said.

And as for sweet potatoes, the market stallholder advised him to buy ordinary spuds and cover them with sugar. It was a town of jokers, and Morg thought it had all gone too far when he turned up shattered at the bus-stop. He waited for ages to begin with. The time-table bore no relation to reality. 'Carless in Cwmtaff' he moaned internally. He knew nothing and everything about the bus service, because he'd worked in Transport at the time of de-regulation, successfully dismantling his own department – so that he had somewhere to go: another department. He knew nothing because, until now, he never had occasion to travel by bus.

Bob's Buses served his area of Cwmtaff, the village of Carreg, above town. It was one of the few remaining small companies. Bob lived in Carreg. Morg knew him from the local Social Club. Bob was the most popular man in the village. Morg couldn't work out why until he saw one of Bob's buses pick up a group of men at closing time outside the Club and ferry them to a place of more liberal opening hours.

When the bus eventually turned up, it bore the legend 'Millie Bus' on the outside. It was a brand new vehicle, nothing like the jalopies Bob usually ran, which Morg frequently passed straining up and

41

down Carreg hill. Morg blinked at the name with astonishment. He was even more astounded when he noticed the logo: a terrapin!

Bob was driving, sitting slouched and smoking right next to a 'No Smoking' sign.

'Wha's up, Mr Owells? Yew look gobsmacked . . . like the new bus, eh? My partner's idea. Ee gets thin's done real quick. Ew might know im.'

'Bob? . . . What? . . . Amazing . . . yes! . . . Who? . . . I mean, why Millie for goodness' sake? It's my . . .'

'I tol yew. Mr Biffen come up with it. Good one, I reckon an all. Millie . . . Millennium, see? Not too shewer 'bout the terrapin mind.'

'I think I can answer that!'

As he dressed for the great post-Millennium event at the Leisure Centre, Morgan reflected on a hectic year since he'd first agreed to take on the project. He wrestled with the black dicky-bow. He would've settled for a suit, but Moffatt insisted on the formal.

His shark-like terrapin had slowly devoured all the other creatures in the tank. Margaret had fortunately given up fish recipes, as he'd refused to eat fish after the dreaded squid. His daughter Liz mercifully hadn't been arrested at any demo's, though she'd occasionally taken to the trees on the Common. It was probably training for some future eco-war, but as long as it occupied her, Morgan ceased to care. Anyway, she appeared to be a changed person recently and had even decided to attend tonight's Vacufashion Show, the first in history.

'Cufflinks! Why had Man invented them? It was

for people who couldn't be bothered to sew on buttons when they came off!'

Since Millie had arrived he had definitely become a very different person. He'd ceased to blame the terrapin for its voracious appetite. It was, after all, a question of eat or be eaten.

Ray Biffen's Millie Buses had thrived and even snatched other routes. Poor old Bob had been forced out due to complaints about the smoke. He found a corner of the Club, surrounding himself in booze and ash.

Margaret did a lot of her shopping in Brecon and Morg was pleased she could find things like butternut squash there. She came home full of vitality and with gleaming eyes. He could never work out the sheer passion these women found in the mundane pursuit of shopping.

He splashed himself with an aftershave called 'Lust' of all things! A Christmas present from Marg and maybe a hint.

'Made from the scrapin's o' bulls' scrotoms,' she colourfully explained.

They took a taxi to the Leisure Centre and Morgan wasn't surprised it was owned by Millietax.

'I should've brought Millie,' he said to Marg and Liz. 'After all, she started the whole thing.'

Liz had shown enormous interest in the huge and very powerful Vacu-terrapin. She was constantly asking questions and even wanted to see the design which Hoovers had come up with so efficiently and promptly.

'One thing's for certain,' he told them, 'the

Vacufins won't go the same way as the C5. It's going to be a great success.'

Morgan's choir – the Penôl Male Voice – went on first and did a selection of their more traditional repertoire. Morgan sang his guts out. This was his night and he wanted to be part of everything.

Damien King turned out to be a lovely man, full of charm and quite down-to-earth. When Liz was introduced to him during the interval, Morg feared the worst. Not only did she not mention 'fur' and 'animal slayer', but she was engrossed in a discussion about the old school and all their former teachers.

The *Western Press* took a photo of Morgan with his arm round one of the models. To his surprise she was no stick insect, but quite busty and had shapely thighs. He hoped the newspaper wouldn't come up with too crass a headline however.

It was all going most smoothly. Some models paraded along the catwalk wearing King's latest creations. The crowd wowed them all. Ray Biffen got to be a judge because his travel company had paid for the expensive buffet afterwards. Biffen's eyes were on sticks!

The moment of truth approached and Morg gripped his wife's hand. Liz had gone missing and he supposed she was backstage with King, so famously had they got on. Morg knew that King's next designs had been tailored especially for the event. TV cameras had arrived to capture this unique happening. Morgan beamed at his wife, who was looking forward to picking holes in the buffet.

Although he was extremely anxious and excited,

he had time to think about Millie, at home in her tank, in splendid isolation. He hardly noticed Richard Moffatt at the mike, thanking him for all his hard work and calling upon him to introduce the final item, a real spectacular.

He was in a daze when he took the mike. The faces swam in front of him.

'I'd like to thank Mr Moffatt for giving me this opportunity. Cwmtaff may be a year late, but we'll outstrip anywhere else. Above all, I'd like to thank Millie, my pet terrapin, who has made everything possible. I just wish she could be here tonight. But, never mind, we have her larger cousin, ready to perform wonders. Please enjoy an event to remember for the rest of your lives.'

Next to the catwalk, a large plush curtain was pulled open, revealing the Vacufins. People were curiously impressed and whispered questions. It had a firm shell worthy of Millie herself. Out from its mouth a vast pipe emerged like an overgrown eel. The Vacufins was switched on and it began to rumble and groan like an ordinary vacuum-cleaner, only multiplied many times.

As the suction increased, on came King in cream shoes to cymbals of applause. He bowed and ushered on the first of his models. There were whistles and yahoos of approval at her fish-dress. As each model appeared the shiney, scaly nature of the evening's theme was revealed. To Morgan Howells, it was as if all his dead fish had been re-born in the form of these exquisite women.

Suddenly, there was a tremendous surge of power

45

from the Vacufins. Handbags flew across the stage and were sucked into the pipe which swung this way and that like an elephant's trunk. The models' accessories were dragged into the nozzle with a jangle and grating of ear-rings and bracelets, and were devoured by the machine. At first, the audience laughed nervously, believing it to be part of the show.

But as the models started to panic and screech, the crowd joined in. Morgan felt himself sucked towards it and clung to his seat. Others were launched over the top, hands frantically reaching out for anything to grab. The scene resembled a mini-twister let loose in a building, as Margaret was flung onto Biffen's lap and he held onto her as they tumbled together in a tangle onto the floor.

Morgan watched in utter horror as the models' expensive, perfectly-designed outfits were ripped from their bodies and ended up in rags in the whirlwind of the Vacufins. His earlier word about 'outstripped' pounded with the growl of the machine. Just as the models themselves, together with the star guest King himself, were being pulled towards the nozzle like filings towards a magnet, it was switched off.

Most of the crowd fell back into stunned respectability, gathering their limbs and belongings as best they could. Morg's wife did not appear however and nor did Ray Biffen. He feared they had been injured seriously.

From behind the edge of the curtains, his daughter Liz emerged to observe the results of this disaster.

Semi-naked models had retreated rapidly, but King in psychedelic tie and boxer shorts was heading straight for Morgan Howells. He was just about to dive-bomb him from the cat-walk, when Liz intervened.

'Dame! Don' blame im. It woz me don' it, arfter all. I don' it f'r all them innocent creatures murdered f' theyr skin an fur yew choose t' ewse on yewer women.'

Morg's marvellous scheme was in ruins. His single instance of creativity had ended in chaos and humiliation. Betrayed by his own family! He vowed to be even more boringly respectable in future (if, indeed, he had any). Moreover, he would ask his wife to find a recipe for terrapin. But when Margaret and Biffen rose from their tumble looking dishevelled and grinning widely, his thought returned to the possibility of a piranha and a tank the size of that disgraced machine.

Allotment for Memories

You wouldn't think these lumps on the earth I'm standing on concealed so much, would you? I mean, they're smooth and firm as a greyhound's back and seem part of the landscape, but really all they are is overgrown slag-heaps.

About a week ago I came here. Sometimes I come to escape, at others just to gaze down on the town and think. The office where I work shrinks to Lego and I wish it could be dismantled as easily. My missis prefers the forestry path. At least it's going somewhere, she'd say. Here, I'm standing still on history, on tons of coal owned by Celtic Power, or whatever they call the company now. That's typical, she would say. But she doesn't know because, the thing is, this is my private place, an allotment for memories. I nurture them carefully. From out of the black-patched moor comes my father, a stern yet guiding presence. His strong sense of the power of history handed down, especially those tales of local heroes defying their Masters, risking all for vital ideals and pennies. If this land were dug up for an opencast mine I'd have to move away.

Yes, last week was definitely escape. We were on the verge of real conflict, where vases would fly and we'd say things we'd later regret, but never admit to being sorry. As always, the week's chores built up, so the house resembled a laundry, dust accumulated so even the spiders moved out in disgust and our carpets had more crumbs than the bird-table.

'Malcolm!' The full name treatment meant TROUBLE. 'Yew don' even notice, d' yew? Yew'd live in a skip if it ad a telly.'

'An 'n aerial . . .'

'Tha's it! Joke! Yewr answer t' ev'rythin! I give up!'

So I ran out here in desperation, stumbling over the tussocky surface, coat half on and shoe-laces undone.

Here, where I couldn't be seen from our back window. My own middle-aged den.

But as I approached these twmps I could hear giggling, sighing and animated chatter. From the top of this tip I peered down to see – in brazen daylight – a young couple canoodling. Well, they were more than canoodling, I'd say, because he was on top of her and both were shedding clothes faster than skinny-dippers. I glimpsed his hand scurrying like a small animal finding a warm resting place.

I breathed heavily from the exertion and both of them stopped their antics to stare in my direction. A bird rose from behind me – a meadow pipit, I believe – and they seemed to ignore me, following its flight and song for a moment before resuming.

I rushed away downhill, alongside the course of one of the many streams. I headed for what is known locally as 'The Chartists' Stone', though my father believed it had nothing to do with them. It's a large, incongruous boulder, like something deposited during the Ice Age. You could certainly imagine those Chartists orating from its natural platform, but to me it was a point of contact with my son. (He was away at uni., and too busy making enough money to survive during holidays; so we didn't see him often). When he was a toddler we'd go there to play 'King of the Castle.' I remember once tumbling downslope so authentically that he chased after me, concerned and calling 'Dad, dad! Yew okay? I didn' urt yew, did I?' After I got up, laughing, he decided to try the same ploy. However, he failed to stop himself rolling and I chased after him, only just catching hold before he fell into a brook.

On my way back, I approached these tips warily, drawn to the possibility of that couple, yet not wanting them to discover me spying and think me some 'dirty old man'. That vision disturbed me, as if I'd seen it on some film or in a dream.

As I reached the slight ridge I was both relieved and disappointed to find that they'd gone. I decided to investigate their cwtsh in the hillside, after all it was like they'd invaded my territory. Their clothes were probably smeared by tell-tale coal, which cropped up between the heather and grass and they might arouse suspicions when they got home.

I noticed something lying in the long reeds near where they'd been. Probably a used condom, or some other item of lust. They treated it all like a game, these young people: no notion of the consequences.

Getting closer I made out a fine, old-fashioned headscarf. Were they back in? I certainly hadn't noticed and, having no daughter, was out of touch. Picking it up, I saw it was creamy, delicately-patterned and had a hint of perfume. I smoothed it and whispered 'I wish . . .' as though I could release some genie. I have to admit it, it stirred something in me, its silkiness like a piece of lingerie.

I hid it in my inside coat-pocket. It seemed strangely familiar. Had Shirley Maclaine (my all-time favourite actress) discarded it in the street in *Days of Wine and Roses*, to be ravished by the wind?

When I returned, Rachel had calmed down and now a glowering silence replaced her previous malice. I'd done nothing wrong, but knew I was to blame. I'd been a huge disappointment to her. She'd always desired to get away from this valley, to see other worlds. Now she sat dug-deep in a novel, as I ghosted past without a greeting, knowing talk was pointless.

Upstairs, I took out the head-scarf and held it next to my face, inhaling a feeling of being young, full of vibrancy. I couldn't recall ever having been so adventurous with Rachel. Continents away in thought, Rachel gave me a shock by bursting in and dumping my shirts on our bed.

'Wha? Wherever did you find tha, Malcolm? It carn be! Tha's incredible!'

'Ow? Ow d'yew mean?'

She lifted it and shook it out, reviving it from a deep sleep.

'This Malcolm . . . don' yew remember? Yew bought it f' me in Morgan's, when we woz courtin. I ewsed t' wear it all-a time. Always thought I'd lost it outa back there . . . it's amazin!'

51

'No . . . it woz in a box at the top of the cupboard. I woz lookin f' photos . . . jest came across it by accident.'

She folded it gently, tying it round her greying hair – her fingers assured after all these years.

'Ey, Mal? What 'bout them times we ad together then out on-a moor? Wouldn' be surprised if our David wern conceived . . .'

'Yeah . . . wish I'd-a found a condom.'

'Wha yew on about, Malcolm? It don' mean nothin t' yew, do it?'

She whipped the scarf off, flung it on top of the clothing and, turning, slammed the door shut, leaving me alone.

I'm here on the tip a week later, wondering if that couple will ever return, keeping the scarf with me for company. Again, I walk down the dip to where I saw them and birds rise, startled, behind me.

Realising the Garden

For years he'd just let it grow and tangle, barely containing the thousands of oak leaves which accumulated in corners, formed sludgy mulch in the guttering and blocked the drains, so they smelled like the panwash at Butlin's where he'd worked as a student during holidays. The back lawn had been churned into mud when his kids were younger and neither grass seed thrown nor turf squared down could alter its inevitable return to brown. Willy Loman had a better idea, cultivating a sidewalk: at least there, crazy dreams could flourish. However, a garden required the kind of attention he couldn't afford.

There were always other people's gardens which mattered more. The stone tortoise of the Welche's opposite, allegedly broken in half by his son's rugby ball! The infinitely precious roses of the meticulous Rossers, who refused to return any ball which so much as touched their plants, keeping it in protest till his son Ryan's best friend Tom (whose family owned half the town) went and asked for it. His name already having the necessary pull.

Above all, there was his mother. She was there in the haphazard and the persistent. The rock cactus which spread everywhere and couldn't be removed, the variegated ivy which strangled whatever was near it, and drank up all the light like a thirsty child at the bottle. Particularly, there was this peculiar plant whose flowers (when they came) were scarlet and furious, but whose leaves and muscly stems resembled the rhubarb. His mother would've known the name, of course. This was a plant which dominated, its arms pushing out and thrusting.

His mother *was* gardens. From the long and practical vegetable one of their council house (a legacy of wartime), to the neat, limey plot of their first mortgaged terrace. The compost heap, the rows of peas and that incredible peach tree in the less erratic climate and chalky soil of the east of England. Peaches from East Anglia! Surely a miracle.

She was an expert cultivator, but also a thief. Trips to the Botanical Gardens in the city invariably bore fruit. The tiniest of cuttings would be slipped into her ready bag, soon taking root along borders, across rockeries or in shaped beds.

Yet when he recalled her digging, it brought back her anger. It was as if the earth itself had committed some terrible sin and was being punished. When he began on the clay of his own back lawn, however, he understood something of her venom. It wasn't like soil at all: it was stubborn as flesh and the root outcrops of the oak were close to the surface, quaking his bones as the spade struck.

He'd lost contact. As soon as he had a wife and children he was no longer hers alone, to be guided. His wife was a rival to be envied, his children reminding her of ageing and of her own mother, the perfect granny she never wanted to be, grey and floury, doting.

His son and daughter joked about the way he'd suddenly discovered the garden. 'Preparing for retirement', they called it, watching his fine hair fall out like the leaves he raked, and its colour two-toned like the ivy he grappled with, tugging at its awkward roots.

The rock cactus could not be destroyed, but it could be contained. The ivy was transplanted to the back fence where it could compete with bramble and bindweed on equal terms. But that unsightly rhubarb flower his wife hated so much had to go.

You couldn't divorce your parents. However many grounds you had – brutality, rejection, or other offspring (such as cats!) they acquired in your place – there was no easy way out. In a shambling way, they'd tried to raise you: though he knew his mother only cared out of guilt. He'd been a responsibility from the start. A classic mistake. Product of a burst condom, he'd been told. If there was affection, then she never picked up the 'phone to express it, hint at it in her polite but cold letters, or even suggest a meeting. She could die and he wouldn't notice it. It sounded callous, but it was true.

Yet he did feel some gratitude, though he wasn't exactly sure what for. Perhaps it was the music she played, the shocking ideas she'd relished expressing in company, or more likely the freedom to roam she'd given him, denied to so many others.

He'd learnt from her how to steal. He was Biff with the golden pen. Bricks for their garden path and

55

books for his restless mind. Absurd items like postcards, just for the dare of it. A challenge. Lucky he was never caught till college and a drunken foray into the back of a hotel, after more alcohol. That was his moment of realisation, when he told himself 'Enough!'

He attacked the rhubarb flower in the raised border at the front with a fork, hacking away at its tough roots. Its large leaves spanned out, for protection almost. It clung to the shallow soil like a dying woman to the last spoonful. The stems were gnarled like hands and feet deformed by bunions and corns. They bled a dribble of white sap as he skewered them. Right down to the last memory he dug deep, flinging its remains over the back fence and into the gentle stream where, for all he cared, it could grow wild. As he did so he noticed a strange blackness around the thick stems, rings of rotting, so unlike the circles of a tree's growth. Below the leathery leaves, a fungus.

Christmas, Easter and birthdays: cards and presents in meaningless rituals. In the end, Willy Loman had confessed to loving his son Biff. What he'd endeavoured to plant could never grow between the apartment blocks. Now there was green, however sparse, and heather spidering outwards and flowers discovered like new stars. He would write her the news, but it would be nothing more than a list.

Schuhmacher's Collapse

Herr Dieter Schuhmacher suddenly collapsed in front of his class of thirteen-year-olds. Their loud jabbering ceased and for a while they stared towards the prostrate man in disbelief. They waited to see if he would get up. Andreas Diebels was the first pupil to make a move. He scurried to the front of the Art Room and stood over the teacher with a smile of triumph. The small, scruffy-haired boy looked up at the class and announced:

'Herr Schuhmacher is dead! That means a day off!'

* * *

Herr Schuhmacher had liked his flat until just recently, when strange things began to happen. After all, he did have a large studio in the attic in which to paint and not many blocks of flats could offer such a facility. His wife Beate was always on about moving to a house in the countryside one day. But they couldn't afford one at present and anyway he found the countryside around Rheinstadt to be boringly man-made. The endless fir and pine forests were monuments to an obsession with Order for its own sake. Man must contain Nature through a vision of it on canvas and not through tampering with it on such a wide scale.

One evening his daughter Uta had rung from Scotland. She'd urged him to visit them that very summer. There was, she'd explained, the possibility of her husband getting a post at a university in Canada and so it might be Herr Schuhmacher's last chance to see her at Edinburgh. He had told her that they'd try to get over. Beate was excited by the prospect of seeing her daughter's family. They both loved Uta so much. Her birth had been so difficult for Beate that they'd decided not to have another child. All their affection was centred on her.

That night they had a few liqueurs before going to bed. Dieter was tired and soon went to sleep while his wife sat up and read a novel.

In the middle of the night he woke up feeling very sick. He put it down to the liqueurs until Beate also began to stir.

'Dieter! What's that odd smell?' she asked, opening her eyes at once (though she was normally slow to wake).

He thought of the plant they'd recently bought. He got up, went to the window-sill and sniffed at its loping yellow flowers and furry leaves which did seem to give off a dust. There was a smell coming from it, but it wasn't pungent. It was aromatic and almost relieved him of the nauseous one which now filled the room.

'It definitely isn't the plant,' he said.

Beate got out of bed, her long nightdress catching in her legs.

'I must have some water immediately,' she said, making for the kitchen.

He noticed a peculiar luminous quality to the air in their bedroom. He quickly opened a window. He drank in the air through the window in great gulps. Dieter went to see if his wife was alright. She was bent over the sink, balancing herself with her plumpish hands fixed to either side of it.

'Dieter! I feel terrible!'

'Quickly! Go to the balcony door,' he advised.

As he helped her by taking one arm, he thought he heard a scuffling of feet outside the door of their flat. He practically dropped his wife into a chair and ran out of the kitchen. He looked at the light under the door in case he might see shadows passing across it. He thought he heard someone going down the stairs, but was too afraid to pursue the noise. He returned to the kitchen, thrust open the balcony door at the end of it and peered down. He saw nothing. But there was a wide ledge over the entrance, so whoever it was could easily have escaped without being seen.

Beate inhaled the air in large doses.

'What is it, Dieter? What does this all mean?'

She was very scared, her eyes jittering. He felt more calm for looking at her.

'I don't know,' he replied, 'maybe some kids from school. They are playing games perhaps . . . Beate, please don't fret. We will sleep alright now. Whoever it was will not return. I feel sure I disturbed them.'

He stroked her greying hair. She got comfort from him and went back to bed. He went quietly to the flat door, moving the catch with extreme care. Slowly, he edged the door open. He peeped outside, expecting to find some evidence of a practical joke there, but there was nothing.

Who could it have been? Andreas Diebels and his

friends were capable of such things, but were too young. They had locked the windows in his classroom and let stink bombs off, but they would hardly go out at night.

Beate was sitting up with her dressing-gown on when he went back to bed.

'Go to sleep, my dear,' he said. 'There'll be no more games, I'm sure.'

They left the windows open. As he lay there in the dark, he couldn't help noticing the luminosity of the air. Was that caused by some sort of gas? Was it a message to him? You couldn't bury the past: it appeared with a force of its own at times. He didn't feel it rise like guilt. He had been young and didn't feel responsible for Hitler's acts. He felt it rise like the subconscious, coming when you were most vulnerable, asleep at night.

A dark March day. The unrelieved grey of the sky seemed flat and tedious as the Niederrhein landscape. He was thinking of Edinburgh as the class were busy drawing cartoons. He wanted so much to be there with his grand-daughter Sandra, flying a kite in the park, to hear her funny questions and try to answer in his broken English.

'Grandpa, why is grass green?' once she'd asked.

'Not always,' he'd replied.

'But it is, Grandpa.'

'Have you seen this grass dead?'

There were things he didn't like about Britain. The last war was always on television. Men talked about it in pubs as if it happened last week. It seemed like a drug to them. The Holocaust was irrelevant: they pumped themselves with their victory. Addicted to the past, they hallucinated about the present. And so, some thought of him as a Nazi!

Yelling at the back of the class broke his reverie. Stefan and Ulrich were flicking ink and taunting each other. He stood up.

'Hey! At your age! You should know better! I will talk to your parents about this.'

The two tall boys stopped their pranks and looked at him. They grinned at him, then sat down muttering, 'Okay' – as if they were doing him a personal favour. Soon the bell went and he was glad to leave the Gymnasium. Today was a good day: he finished at 12.30. As he walked towards the car park he saw that his Mini wasn't where he'd parked it but was actually in the road. Who could do such a thing?

'The bloody shitheads!' he shouted.

The car had been placed at an angle, its rear end jutting out dangerously into the road. It was surprising the police hadn't noticed it. He paced around his red Mini tapping it and cursing as he circled it.

'The police must see to this. The kids have minds of shit!'

For some reason someone in the school was persecuting him. Again he thought of Andreas Diebels. This boy had so much evil in him. He once made the whole class refuse to answer questions. They all just sat there as he gazed proudly on them as though they were machines he'd invented and could work by remote control. But no, he and his allies were too small to do this thing.

Herr Schuhmacher ran back to the school, his heart sending surges of anger through him. He cut his way through a jungle of amazed children's faces. Herr Kreis shouted 'Dieter!' at him and he showed the man a clenched fist and kept repeating, 'The shitheads! The shitheads!' He leapt up the school stairs, hearing the tittering of younger pupils chase him all the way to the Principal's office. He knocked on the door with such ferocity that he thought he'd damaged his knuckle. Sweat sprung from his forehead in geysers. He wheezed with every breath like an asthmatic.

The Principal, Herr Keppler, opened the door. He was puffing calmly on his pipe.

'Herr Keppler . . . I've had enough . . . they are pigs . . . my car!'

'Please, come in and sit down, Herr Schuhmacher,' said Keppler in a slightly patronising tone of voice.

Dieter was glad to sit down. He tried to steady himself by taking deep breaths.

'Now tell me, Herr Schuhmacher, what's going on?' Keppler was curiously amused. Dieter felt the man was relishing the situation.

'Well, Herr Keppler, I went to the car park only to find my Mini in the road. Somebody has shifted it over the pavement and into the road with the hand-brake on. God knows what damage has been done. It must have happened during break. This has gone too far! I'm going to get the police in.'

'A minute, Herr Schuhmacher . . .'

Keppler was still completely at ease, blowing smoke-rings.

'No. I have made up my mind. I will take these pupils to court.'

'I think we can settle the matter internally, Herr Schuhmacher. We will find out who did this and they will compensate you fully from class funds.'

'Money! Huh! It's all a question of money is it? Well that does not satisfy me, I can tell you. It is a question of human decency.'

Dieter got up and strode out of the Principal's office. Everything could be bought off in Germany today, even a man's total humiliation. When he was young he'd predicted it in his cartoons. There was the one with the woman in a fur coat waiting for her limousine while children turned the world of cars, dogs and trees upside down around her. He had sensed it then. Now it had actually happened.

The days passed and Herr Keppler had no success in finding the culprits. Dieter had become obsessed by his hunt. He lay awake at night, waiting for a telling sound. He kept asking the more pleasant pupils at school whether they had seen anything during their breaktime. He was convinced that the incidents with the gas and the car were related. The face of Andreas Diebels kept returning to him, with its rodent-like features and hair which spiked in all directions. The boy was quite quiet in class and when Dieter asked him a question he would just sneer back with contempt. What was the point of confronting a boy like that with crimes he may have committed? If he spoke at all he would simply deny it or look at Dieter as though he were a half-wit.

In the Staff Room he expressed his fears to Herr Koch, a history teacher who was a good listener.

'Yes, you're right about Diebels,' said Koch, 'but he has had a bad upbringing. His parents are divorced and his mother, with whom he lives, doesn't give a damn about him.'

'Really? But even so I cannot excuse the boy. He doesn't seem to have a lot of good in him.'

'He is interested in history.'

'Yes? You surprise me. What period, may I ask?'

'Well . . . Bismarck mostly. But he does ask me a lot of questions about Hitler. Of course we don't cover that period too much. He did a terrible thing to Herr Beckman once, you know.'

'What was that?'

'Why, he gave the poor man a written contract predicting the day of his death. The whole class had signed it. Beckman was most perturbed.'

Dieter felt deeply sorry for Beckman. He was prone to long bouts of depression and should never have gone in for teaching.

After school that day, Dieter went to see the Principal to ask how investigations were going. Herr Keppler told him that he'd spoken to the senior classes and asked that the culprits should go to Dieter and apologize at once. This angered Dieter who demanded that every boy he taught in the upper school be interviewed, but Keppler would have none of this and suggested that Dieter was getting it all out of proportion.

The next day was Friday and the lesson before break he taught 8B, Diebels's class. Their noise was appalling. He was overcome by the pointlessness of it all as he stood, ignored, at the front. Bettina Schultz was eating a sandwich. Peter Stein was demonstrating intricate drum-rhythms to his friend Reiner by beating two rulers on the desk. Diebels was lounging in a relaxed manner, reading a magazine.

'Be quiet!' he yelled.

They looked up at him, stunned for a moment by the volume. All, that is, except Diebels who remained flicking through his magazine.

'Andreas!' The boy didn't look up, so Dieter walked over to him. Dieter took hold of the magazine, tearing a page in the process. At last Diebels looked up and waved his hand at the magazine as if nothing mattered to him.

'It wasn't that interesting anyway.'

Dieter was speechless. He felt a beaten man and returned to the front of the class as if that would restore his authority.

'Today we're going to do some posters . . .'

'Not posters again!' they grumbled in unison.

Their noise began to increase. It spread through the class like a rapid infection. He looked at Diebels pathetically, almost asking for help. The boy's face filled a frame in his head. He felt gas pumped through his body from his head. Blood was sucked into his heart like dust into a vacuum-cleaner. The gas replaced it in every vein, making his limbs weak. As he fell, the ceiling burst with a light like a blast of a shell in the distance. His body became a balloon that was pricked by the falling masonry he thought came down on him. The gas escaped from him and into the room where he lay, unconscious.

Changing the Script

The director Bryn took her to one side afterwards. His eyes were wide with sympathy, but she still felt inadequate.

'Look, Rhian, I'm really sorry. I know it's a small part, but it's right for you . . . there'll be another chance next year, I'm sure.'

Always next year. It was what she'd been told since attending these workshops and at school as well, where doing GCSE drama hadn't even improved things.

'I aven' got the right figure, ave I?'

'Don't be silly. That's nothing to do with it.'

She peered, searching lies. It wasn't only that, but other things she couldn't mention. Stephanie given the main role and her father working in the Beeb. Her accent too, that Valleys scar which couldn't be erased. She wanted to confront Bryn and watch him squirm, then she remembered her mother's words, 'I's like tha love . . . oo yew know.' She walked away from him without her cheery 'S'long!'

Meeting her mam to go shopping in Cardiff; her anger came gushing . . . 'I'm bloody sick of it, mam. Think I'll pack it in, onest. A chicken in *Animal Farm*, a bloody tart in *Oliver* and now this . . . a fat friend oo's practiclee a chocoholic! Why do I bother?"

'I know, love. An I bet yewer better than tha Stephanie. Look at-a Stereoglyphics, ey done it.'

'Phonics mam.'

'Yeah, they might elp an all!'

Her mam was like a friend, but she couldn't get it right. She could give Rhian a cwtsh and was always there for her, though the encouragement never convinced her. Boys who fancied her only wanted one thing – and that wasn't help with their homework, unless it was Personal & Social Ed. Her mam tried not to favour Rhian's brother Chris, but it was obvious that she did and this made Rhian very jealous.

As ever, she tried on all the wrong clothes. In River Island, a skimpy dress her mam could've fitted into when pregnant, made her legs stand out like tree trunks. She tried in vain to cheer her up.

'I know, le's get some marzipan in Thornton's . . . whoops!' She gulped back the gaff seeing Rhian's expression. Her mother's handbag drew Rhian's attention and thoughts away from her own problems.

'Come on, mam. Le's go an look f'r an andbag f'yew. I think tha one belongs in St Fagans.'

The tattered brown bag hung from her like a mouldy coconut. She laughed and her mam reluctantly agreed, always wary of spending money on herself. So they searched in the handbag department of every store for one not too expensive, not too plasticky, big or small, with a short thin strap and definitely not smelling of leather, till they ended up roughly where they'd begun, in the precinct. They went into the Handbag Shop, an obvious choice they'd neglected.

67

Her mam proceeded to pull the padding out of numerous bags to try them for size, with her purse, brush and other essentials. Rhian kept her distance, especially when Stephanie Marshall entered, complete with tanned, open-shirted boyfriend.

'This seems orright, Rhi. What d'yew think?' Her mam hailed her in an embarrassingly loud voice. Padding was strewn everywhere. Stephanie was browsing, sniffling, her hunk in tow. She spotted Rhian and smiled, nodding, 'Hi!' Her boyfriend caught round her as if to steer her away.

'Le's go, mam!'

She stomped off before her mam could protest, out into the precinct.

'Rhian! Rhian!' Her mam followed, calling after her as if she was an escaped toddler. The shop alarm was triggered, and her mam stood shock-still, a stolen handbag full of her belongings in her hand. Rhian took pity on her and turned back into the shop just as Steph and her Romeo appeared smirking. She wished she was an infant again, so she could dart into the crowd and be lost. Luckily, she explained the situation to an understanding manager, and they had no choice but to buy that bag. Stephanie had seen her. She could never return to drama now.

In the car later, Mrs Griffiths was furious. 'I don' care oo yew seen. Sort yewrself out! . . . I jest wish yew ad a dad around t'back me up.'

'A father, but not im, mam?'

'I tol yew. Ee wuz a slob.'

She clammed up, brooding. Her mam had never

really explained. He'd walked out because he was such a kid, chasing other women, out with the lads. That was it. The rest she had to imagine.

That night she even dreamt of Stephanie. It was becoming an obsession. In the studio together, she and Steph were dressed for Judo, opposite each other, bowing. She let out the Banshee yell and broke all the rules, flattening her. It was more like sumo wrestling as she thought, 'At least my flab's good f'summin!' while two security guards (like the ones from the precinct) dragged her off her adversary, who lay on the floor whimpering. As she was marched off, Bryn ran up to her screaming, 'You're finished! That was a trust game!'

She felt exhilarated when she woke, until Chris's annoying whistling brought her down to earth. He was so wiry and could scoff just as much as he liked. She didn't want to play stodgy Gloria, longed to take Steph's part: weird and wild, yet funny at the same time. There was a small photo of herself on a shelf dressed as a Red Indian, chubby and ruddy but totally content. She vaguely recalled her dad playing with her, hiding behind the sofa pursued by soldiers as their buffalo grazed in the hall.

Her dad warning, 'They're goin t' slaughter ower buffalo, love!'

'No, dad, we carn let em win!'

Later, she had a real barney with Chris and he called her 'fat bitch'. Her mam took his side because she'd kicked him. She went on hunger strike all day, forcing her mam into pangs of guilt. She couldn't be anorexic though, she loved her food, especially the

69

spicey stuff. Her mam went on about this artist Rodin and his nude sculptures. Maybe fashions would change.

School brought her out of herself. Her friend Trish was even more buxom and didn't seem to care whatever. Rhian drew strength from her determination. Trish was a match for any snotty boy's comments.

'Oi! Ippo bum!'

'Wha d'yew wan', welly-merchant? Wool on yewr flies, or wha?'

Trish could get a PhD in Insultology. She was the expert, and Rhian her apprentice. Coping was one thing, motivation another: and by next Saturday's drama workshop she hardly knew her lines and told her mam she was too shattered to go.

'I think yew'll find thin's ave improved,' Mrs Griffiths insisted. She sounded as if she knew something. Rhian didn't pursue it, but went along with her as always.

Stranger than strange, Bryn actually greeted her and Steph wasn't to be seen. She was dying to ask Beth (who went to Steph's school) but she didn't want to appear concerned. After warm-up exercises, Bryn got them together, explained that Stephanie had had an accident and he'd like 'Rhian Griffiths' to take the main role. For a moment she assumed there must be another Rhian Griffiths, till she noticed the bemused faces focussed on her.

Amazingly, there were no protests and she nodded modestly. The dream: did she possess extraordinary powers? Was she some kind of witch maybe?

They read the first part of the script. She couldn't

70

concentrate, but tried to put every emotion into the part. Jo was highly strung, brilliant, yet loathed both her parents. Her father was having an affair, her mother lived for work, not realising she was being cheated. Jo found out, relishing the combat she created between her parents. A great part, though she still felt on trial, or worse, a substitute.

When Bryn spoke to her afterwards, she expected him to be hypercritical.

'Rhian! You did fine . . . you know, your mother's a great lady!'

'Eh? Wha?'

'I talked to her on the phone the other night . . . didn't she tell you?'

'No!'

'She said you were out. She explained how ambitious you are, when I told her Steph had broken her leg. She's very persuasive, you know.'

They were in the corridor outside the studio. She stopped dead.

'Bryn! Yew didn give me the part coz of er, did yew?'

'No way, Rhian. I was considering you anyway . . . but, given your background, I thought you'd be ideal.'

'Ow d'yew mean? Wha's she said?'

But he avoided the answer and busied himself with a swift 'Bye!'

In the car home she confronted her mam.

'Why aren' yew more pleased, love?'

'What did yew tell im, mam? Bout me, bout ower famlee?'

'I seen a script when I woz tidyin yewer room.

71

Couldn elp it . . . well, it woz a bit like yewer dad, that sod avin a bit-on-a-side.'

'Thanks a lot, mam.'

'I on'y done it f'yew.'

'An ow am I goin t'lose two stone f' the performance, eh? Chop off a couple o'limbs?'

Mrs Griffiths nearly veered off the road, they laughed so much. The first time together for weeks.

She was riled by her mother, but knew she could do it: put on Jo's accent and manipulate people as she did. As rehearsals progressed though, certain lines didn't fit. The dumpy friend Gloria was now played by a less dumpy girl, and Jo's boyfriend – played by an arrogant boy called Paul – was uncomfortable complimenting her on her loveliness. Bryn even suggested changing 'radiance' to 'attraction' and he wasn't joking.

He reassured Rhian they'd pad up Gloria and make-up would perform wonders on her face. She enquired if they could manage a facelift!

She did feel that she was becoming Jo, however. So much so that Chris began to moan about her 'snobby voice'. She slipped into character without realising.

'Mother! You're always working. Why can't you relax?'

'Workin? Part-time down-a Spar?'

Except that there was no father to practise on. He'd gone, jumped the script. She spoke to him in her head: 'I know all about you. I saw you with her, so don't deny it! Of course I won't tell Mother, but you must agree to help me a little bit more.'

72

Two nights before the dress rehearsal she had another clear dream. Her dad appeared, a cross between Bryn and Siôn (who played Jo's dad). They were walking down a railway track. She was little and dressed only in her knickers. She felt so ashamed. Rhian pulled free and he strode on into the dark, never looking back. She could hear a train coming. When she shouted, 'Daddy!', he'd disappeared. She rolled off the track and woke up, glad to have her nightie on.

She puzzled over this. After the dream about Steph, she wondered if there was an important secret about her dad. The dream still plagued her. The make-up did allay some fears: not a butterfly, but a colourful moth. She was confident of every scene except the one where she had to talk dirty to Ross, Jo's boyfriend. The lines sounded perfect coming from Jo: 'Ross, I want you to do it like I saw my father doing it. Do you think you can manage that?' It wasn't shyness, because they were disturbed at the crucial moment. During dress rehearsal, when Paul froze, she knew it was her fault. He didn't say his line. Bryn was furious.

'What the hell's going on?'

'She can't relax! It was different with Steph!'

'Both of you, loosen up and grow up! Take it from Jo's line about you managing. The bloody writer must've known.'

They forced themselves along and Rhian even bit Paul on the ear. This made Paul's energy and childishness come alive in his character and Bryn even complimented them on their improvisation after.

She was enjoying being Jo. For once, in control of her destiny and with a boy to lick her feet.

She was less afraid on the night. All the others were wound up backstage, bantering like a group of DJs. Rhian felt strangely calm and as the drama progressed it took her over completely. Even the abridged sex scene was acted with gusto. Nearing the finale things began to fall apart, because of her over-confidence. She started to alter the lines. She had a sense of someone particular watching from the audience. Her changes threatened the play's logic.

'Ross, my father . . . he hasn't gone away . . . he's dead, you know . . .' She strove to correct herself. 'I mean, it's as if he's dead . . .'

Paul was thrown. He continued, more mechanically.

It was as though someone spoke through her and the play had become one of her dreams. When she transformed the last lines to, 'I'll not let him haunt me. I don't need parents anyway!' it was heresy, yet the applause was resounding. As she took a bow, there in the second row she saw Steph sitting next to a middle-aged man. Rhian stared at him, aghast. It couldn't be . . . it was impossible!

Backstage, Bryn cwtshed her at the same time whispering 'Why the hell did you change those lines, Rhian? You nearly blew the whole show!'

Jo was finished. She'd never play her again. She rubbed the make-up off slowly and carefully. How could Jo reject her family? There was a knock on the door.

'Come in!'

Steph hobbled in on crutches, followed by the man. If only he . . .

'My dad! . . . You were utterly brill, Rhian. And I loved the improvising. It made Jo seem more humane. Did Bryn suggest that?' She kissed her on the cheek. Her dad handed Rhian the bouquet. She was delighted and feeling generous.

'I didn even look like er. Yew'd ave bin much better Steph . . .'

'The way things are going, I can see futures for both you girls,' her dad said, and he sounded sincere.

'Rhian, you were great, honestly. I'll see you at the workshop when I get rid of these props.'

As they turned to leave, Steph added, 'By the way, was that your mother in the Handbag Shop? She looked a real character and a laugh. I can see who you take after.'

In the car home, her mam was full of praise. She kept repeating how glad she was that Rhian wasn't 'like tha silly bitch Jo.'

'I cocked up the endin, mam!'

'I know, love. Bryn tol me arfta. Ee woz quite 'pecific mind.'

Mrs Griffiths eyed Chris to check that he was asleep in the back. She fell quiet, sighing occasionally.

'Rhi, love?'

'Wha mam?'

'It worries me!

'What does?'

75

'Y'know, why yew never tol me before, tha yew knew bout him.'

'Mam! Yew never tol me the truth did yew?'

'I did, Rhi. Well, as much as I could.'

Rhian gazed into the distance, up valley towards her town. The confusion over what she dreamed and what was real met when the road followed the railway line. At that point there was a tunnel through the mountain. She'd never noticed it before.

In Enemy Territory

They had a lift to Tates Avenue. Sean, Pat and Glyn were going to see England play Northern Ireland at Windsor Park. A track of Bruce Springsteen's called '10th Avenue Freeze-out' shuttled back and fore in Glyn's mind, like a black taxi beetling up and down the Falls Road. Only the lyrics were altered to fit the scene . . .

Tates Avenue freeze-out
Tates Avenue freeze-out.

. . . he sang to himself. Sean and Pat started whispering the same as Glyn and his wife did when walking through Ballymena and talking about their hopes for a United Ireland. Glyn, anxious to impress upon them his knowledge of Belfast suggested a remedy.

'We're Jackie, Willy and Sammy, alright?'

The comment started off a string of cracks between Sean and Pat which referred to marked differences between Catholic and Protestant people.

'Their noses are bigger,' said Sean.

'No, our noses are bigger,' replied Pat.

'It's a wonder you two have lived this long, you're that confused,' Glyn butted in.

Sean and Pat stared straight ahead of them, just in case someone from the window of a terraced house spotted the size of their noses and actually knew if they were too big or too small. Glyn, however, whose face was more leprechaunish than either of the other two, looked into house windows and stopped at a lamp post.

'So this is a Protestant lamp-post!' he addressed it.

'Sssssh!' said Sean, 'watch out for Linfield fans now.'

'I'm from the Malone Road,' said Pat.

'I'm not from England,' added Glyn.

This definitely wasn't the Falls. For a start there was no litter, no imaginative graffiti and an absence of bricked-up houses and troops. The houses looked as if they were lived in by people who had jobs. Glyn had heard the polished door-steps of these terraces and the litter in the Falls used in theological arguments. Claims were made that a kind of Medieval war was being waged in the province in which the doorsteps represented a Protestant work ethic and the litter a lack of individual initiative on the part of the people subservient to Rome. Yet how could Catholics have developed a work ethic when they couldn't get work? They had always been banned from working in the shipyards, Short Brothers, Mackies and the like, where your address was your most vital qualification.

Finally, the three young men latched onto a queue of ferocious-looking Glasgow Rangers supporters. Glyn had to remind himself that the match was England against Northern Ireland when he saw all those tam-o'-shanters. Many clutched half-empty bottles of wine, and looked fully-equipped for combat in the skinhead garb of halfmast jeans, braces and 'bovver boots.' The cropped convict haircuts made you think there had been a break-out at the local jail. The three of them avoided getting tangled in this crowd and changed direction for the other end of the ground. For a while they communicated through a subtle series of nods and twitches, afraid in case they should let slip with that fatal name 'Sean' or 'Pat'. It was alright to be the goalie for N. Ireland and be called 'Pat', but standing on the terraces with such a name was different. 'Glyn', of course, was fairly neutral, and could even be classified as 'Protestant'.

The streets were full of fans. The warm Saturday and the prospect of seeing Kevin Keegan had brought them out in thousands. Talk rose like bubbles pricked by sharp bursts of laughter. Sean was confiding in Glyn that the best turf in Ireland was to be found in Celtic Park, the ground where Belfast Celtic had once played. It was shipped over from Wembley he said.

The other two left Glyn to stand in the queue for tickets. They seemed gone an eternity, though they were only going to the toilet. What if he were stranded in enemy territory? He began to feel conspicuous, as if the fans brandishing Union Jacks and Ulster flags could read his mind and stamp him as a Catholic sympathizer. He was relieved when they eventually returned.

You just couldn't win, he thought to himself. Visiting shops in the Falls Road or sitting in black taxis huddled up alongside strangers, his wife would insist on talking to him. When she did, he would give her an angry glare as if she'd just insulted him in public. He would prune her sentences with a short, sharp 'Yes!' or 'No!' and then go red as if he really was an SAS under-cover man. As they took their place on the stands, Glyn decided that the best course of action was to address either Sean or Pat quietly and individually.

Pat and Sean were in the midst of an animated conversation over the attributes of various Manchester United players. Sean, being a Manchester United fan, wouldn't have anything said against them.

'Joe Jordan'd be better off advertising dentures than playing football,' said Pat a smile gleaming from his teeth.

'I suppose he scores all those vital goals by trapping the ball in his gums,' retorted Sean in his usual confident manner.

Sean seemed to have few worries in the world. In true Catholic fashion he'd married Glyn's sister-in-law when they discovered she was pregnant. He always seemed to have money to spare. It was a mystery where it came from, but a new stereo unit or the latest fashionable gear were always forthcoming.

Glyn looked round at Windsor Park. It was a ramshackle ground, and reminded him of Edgar Street, Hereford, where he'd seen a famous Cardiff City defeat, but had been pleased to shout 'Kairdiff!' from the terraces. As it filled up, you could almost hear the fencing creak. The two boxes for TV cameras on the stand opposite looked like pigeon-lofts. You could imagine some commentator coo-cooing his banalities from there:

'The atmosphere is set for this Home International

in Belfast'. The excuses if England lose: 'feeling the effects of a long season' and 'an understrength England side'.

The kop to the right of them was packed with chanting masses. The Ulster flag was prominent; a red, bloody hand in the middle of it. Yet there were plenty of Union Jacks. A confused people, these Loyalists. They were also having problems with their chanting. Placing 'Northern Ireland' in the more recent chants borrowed from Spion Kop or Stretford End posed grave problems of scanning. This produced 'Nerrrrrrrn Ireland' with a distinct patriotic emphasis on the 'Ireland' bit. Some disgruntled individuals used poetic licence and shouted for 'Ulster'. 'There's only one Sammy McIlroy' they chanted, as if to drive all the other Sammy McIlroys in Northern Ireland to the brink of suicide.

Sean was standing next to Glyn, smoking a pipe. His boyish features made the pipe look out of place, until you remembered he was the father of a two-month-old baby girl. Pat was looking enviously at the groups of fans who passed in front of them carrying cans of beer and swigging flagons of cider. His mouth was suffering from drought.

'We should've been to an off-licence, Sean.'

He said 'Sean' unwittingly. Glyn gave him a nudge.

'Aye, we should've done, Billy,' he said to Pat, anxious not to alarm any nearby Paisleyites.

The band of the Royal Irish Fusiliers were finally clapped off the field by nearly everyone, after stirring versions of *Una Paloma Blanca* and *Amazing Grace*.

The crowd was ready for battle. Two charming females in T-shirts screamed 'Come on Northern Ireland!' as the team came onto the field. Glyn watched their breasts bounce to the rhythm of the kop's chanting. The one with fair hair caught him looking and he jerked his head upwards, pretending to be looking for someone in the crowd.

Sean became a raving maniac now that the game had kicked off. 'Hammer him, Sammy! Come on, Jimmy, make mincemeat of him, son!' In fact, as Northern Ireland were outpacing England in the early stages of the game, and exploited all England's poor passing and silly errors, Sean was conducting a single-minded revolution. As he shouted, 'Northern Ireland' became 'Ireland!' Glyn began to fear for their safety. Strangely enough the crowd around them didn't seem to notice, though they always prefaced the 'Ireland' with a 'Northern'. To Glyn's amazement, after a good quarter of an hour of this, a few people actually began to let the 'Northern' slip as well. He wondered whether this was an identity crisis or simply an annexation of the South. It certainly wasn't the difficulty of scanning that the kop had faced earlier.

Sean, encouraged by this success, became very caustic in his comments. He told Channon the England striker renowned for his farm in Hampshire to 'Get back to the fields!' and 'Stick to sheep-shagging!' (titters from the T-shirted girls). A fellow heckler joined Sean in a stereo partnership and accused Brooking the subtle midfielder, of forgetting his ballet shoes. Boldness and patriotism reached the point of no return, when Sean urged the ref to 'Get back to Scotland' even 'Get back to Glasgow!' by which time Pat and Glyn had edged a little distance from the ranter, in case the missiles should start flying.

When Northern Ireland scored there was pandemonium. Hugging, kissing . . . Sean turned towards one of the girls with the T-shirts, but actually restrained himself. Glyn was buffeted about like a human pin-ball. 'Easy! Easy!' chanted the crowd, and very soon 'Ireland! Ireland!' This was not annexation, it was invasion! The border had been destroyed. Now, for each player who touched the ball, Sean would repeat his favourite phrase 'No doubt, Sammy! No doubt, Willy!'

'No doubt about what?' Glyn asked, shielding his mouth with a hand.

'No doubt about their skill!' replied Sean.

The ground buzzed like a nest of bees on overtime. As England began to assert their authority on the game, a Cockney accent came from behind them 'Come on England! Get it right!' No one seemed to hear this, but a minute later a slurred voice from the front produced a P. G. Wodehouse voice: 'I say, come on, chaps!'

'Game, set and match,' said Pat, as everyone laughed.

By now, the floodlights were infested with climbing termites. At the very top, one jubilant fan waved a Union Jack, unaware of the irony. A few had also got on top of the stands, leaving their beer-cans littering the terraces along with their inhibitions. A sober warning came over the PA system.

'Would those on top of the Reserved Stand please come down in the interests of their own safety.'

However, this seemed to act as an incentive, and more youths appeared on the roof of the stand, waving their banners. Two red-white-and-blue banners were displayed: the colours of paving-stones around estates in Ballymena. Put there to keep away evil spirits no doubt.

Very soon the RUC arrived to clear up the situation. They dragged off one boy from the ranks of the kop and were greeted with cheers. Two policemen had clambered up onto the Reserved Stand roof, and the match became a background event. Eyes were fixed on them as they moved towards the fans. It wasn't a very accomplished military operation and they kept slipping on the roof. Eventually one policeman grappled with a bare-chested youth and the knotted ball of the two of them disappeared from sight over the edge of the stand. Hardly anyone noticed Keegan hitting the bar for England, because another youth was felled by a policeman, who kicked him while he lay down. There was much applause from the terracing.

'Quite right too!' moaned a snarling man next to Glyn. 'I'd stick 'em all in prison. Bloody hooligans!'

The ref continued to amaze Sean and Pat with his decisions. Pat shook his head in disbelief and Sean growled 'No way, ref! No way!'

'No way what?' Glyn enquired.

'No way was he right,' said Sean, giving Glyn an exasperated look, 'The defence should stop sunbathing, that's what they should do.'

When England scored it was predictable. Even Sean was silenced for a while, as the crowd suffered a communal hangover. During half-time the biggest cheer was reserved for the Irish wolfhound who accompanied the band onto the field and proceeded to excrete in the centre-circle, to the delight of 30,000.

'England have twelve turds on the field now!' said Sean's stereo partner at the start of the second half.

Northern Ireland's despair increased. Their forwards would have been too small for parts in 'Snow White and the Seven Dwarfs', yet the midfield hoisted the ball in the air in their direction. Sean called for substitute 'Big Derek Spence' to be brought on. The two girls echoed him with a shrill chorus of 'Yes! Bring on Big Derek!' The Irish manager's ear-power must have been remarkable, if a little delayed, because with fifteen minutes to go, Derek Spence was sent on. Sean rather lost favour with those girls when Spence failed to score: and England's winner, a few minutes from the end, turned the afternoon sour for the partisan crowd.

'Bring on George Best!' suggested Sean.

'Can't. He's in America,' said his stereo partner.

'Fly over George Best!' Sean added. But it was useless. The final whistle must have sobered up a record number of people. Glyn heard much grumbling as they left the ground. He tried to look as doomed as possible so as not to offend the others.

'Can't believe it!' said Pat, 'They didn't deserve to lose.'

Everybody seemed to be saying variations on that sentence.

They encountered a swarm of Linfield supporters, some of whom doubled up as Rangers fans. Glyn noticed 'UDA', the Protestant terrorist organisation well-known for their social work and sectarian murders, tattooed in large blue letters on one of their arms. Pat and Sean seemed too preoccupied to be scared, and anyway shared the expression of gloom with them. As they reached the corner of Tates Avenue Sean suddenly launched into a verbal attack on England.

'Typical of those bastards! Only won because they scored more goals!'

'It helps!' said Pat.

'We should've scored three in the first quarter of an hour,' Sean went on, 'we were all over them then.'

Two men walking near them backed up Sean's observations.

'England were a load of wankers! We should've beaten them easy, sure.'

The man who spoke was small and dark-haired. He had piercing blue eyes, which were possessed with anger and alcohol.

'As long as Italy hammer them in the World Cup,' said Sean as they walked on.

'Aye, well, I hope they win . . . even though they're Fenian bastards!'

The force of the last two words, set off Sean and Pat's legs in a sudden acceleration. Glyn followed them and didn't look back at the man. They were halfway towards the roundabout before they realised how obvious they'd made it.

'Want to go back and finish the conversation?' said Pat.

Sean looked behind them to see if they had been followed. Walking home was risky. The roundabout was in the middle of wasteland below the motorway. Only Catholics would be walking further than the end of Tates Avenue. You could be picked off as you crossed the road.

'How many Sinn Feiners are there in Italy?' said Glyn.

He could hardly keep up with Sean and Pat's pace now. They were round the corner and into safety. 'This is Provoland' said the graffiti on the corrugated iron walls of Celtic Park Greyhound Stadium. Concrete blocks and yellow ramps marked the spot where the road was sealed off at night. Sean and Pat stopped at a small shop and decided to go in for some pop to drink. Glyn didn't like the idea. He didn't want to ask for it, and even when Sean asked him if he could get him anything, Glyn declined because he didn't want the other two to know his fear. Belfast was the ideal place for paranoia. You could justify every form of it, especially if you were an outsider.

Glyn saw the match factory which made up the parapet of one entrenched community. It had been blown up by the Provisionals, his wife had told him, because only Protestants had been employed there. He imagined that to a General it was an invaluable buffer zone. When they built the motorway, Glyn thought, did they intend it to be a boundary? That day, he had crossed over into enemy territory and returned unscathed. Pat and Sean came from the shop and offered him a swig of pop. They could call each other by their names again. Glyn felt in every way that he was on their side, except when he started speaking.

'No doubt!' he said, as if to contradict his thoughts.

'No doubt what?' asked Sean.

'I've no idea,' said Glyn.

They walked along the Donegal Road at a leisurely pace now. Up above, a helicopter flew, as if waiting for a shooting or bombing incident to happen. He knew exactly what he had no doubt about. He had been collecting evidence that day at Windsor Park. Exhibit A: the match factory.

Dead Hero Silence

Front page of the 'Mirror'. Jason Freeman. He'd committed suicide by taking an overdose of sleeping pills. The photo showed him very dapper in a flowery tie. Not a trace of anxiety there. An impending court case. Training a boys' team. Accused of sexual assault. He'd phoned his brother, famous TV presenter. His brother had put the phone down. Imagine the guilt!

Jason Freeman . . . an early season match at Tormouth and a carful of Bluebirds' fans. Not just any fans, but writers for the fanzine *Fly Bluebirds Fly!* It was the height of fanzine popularity and we were avid scribblers and sellers. A stapled 'zine costing only 30p and the product of Little Mick's imagination and sweat. To prove the true nature of fanzine philosophy he'd actually gone into away fan areas and tried to flog it. Once the police had told him to get out of the Gillingham kraal, or they'd confiscate the lot.

Little Mick sat at the front, next to Mark at the wheel. Mark had connections. He set up interviews with our players and had befriended the captain, Rob Parry. At our end-of-season 'zine awards ceremony at The Mount in Cwmtaff, needless to say Parry was Player of the Year. We had a learned discussion on prejudice in sport. Rob had stated that

89

racism was definitely out, but he couldn't stand gays. They were beyond.

Jason Freeman . . . we didn't even discuss him on the way down.

Next to me in the back was Mark's *brawd*, Paul. Paul was quiet to the point of anonymity, and the last to harm anyone. He lived with his mam and a long-haired spaniel he carried around like a baby. If he hadn't been Mark's brother, he'd have had loads of stick.

Next to Paul sat Big Mick himself. 'The Big Man' as Little Mick dubbed him. He was six foot four and had muscles like a bull. He had a Bluebirds tattoo on one arm and CCFC on the other.

Going down to Tormouth the banter was heightened by cans of Stella. Big Mick drank it like a baby on the bottle.

'I remember Chelsea. They woz always the worse . . . tha time we woz 3–1 up an arf the Chelsea fans left the Canton. Course, we shoulda known. Most o' them missed Kerry Dixon scorin the equalizers!'

'Yeah, it all kicked off with the bricks . . .' prompted Little Mick.

'The whool of the Bob Bank attacked by flyin bricks an then . . . it woz like a fuckin pincer movement . . . two mobs o' Chelsea comin at us.'

'Aye, an one cop with a dog stopped the lot of 'em!' Little Mick finished off the story, as if they were a double act.

The two Micks often talked about violence, without ever admitting they'd taken part. Mark nodded and reminisced how it 'went off' outside

90

Bristol City, in the days when *they* were the enemy not the Jacks. The park outside a perfect place for a battle. Paul kept his head down, supping the lager voraciously and chuckling occasionally.

I felt as if I'd missed out on something, though I had my own memories, which I tentatively volunteered.

'I remember when Portsmouth took the Grange End. For some reason I woz in the Canton nex' t' two Swedish women. I carn think why . . .'

'I can!' quipped Little Mick.

'Do yowr missis know 'bout this?' joked Mark.

The mood inside the car was buoyant, quite the opposite of our season so far, which had been uninspiring, to say the least. We had signed a centre-back who made Big Mick look like a fashion model. His name was Steve Jones, but he wasn't Welsh. He resembled a rugby second-row forward and often played like one.

We arrived at Tormouth quite early and, coincidentally, standing opposite a promenade of hotels, we spotted two of our players. They were like hippos out of water in their over-sized suits. Why do footballers always wear those? Is it to make them look bigger off the field? One was a tall, gangling centre-back (who would probably be sub) and the other our wiry, hard-working black striker. Mark stopped and rolled the window down. We shouted, made bold by booze.

'Ey Ga', ey Jon! We gonna win, eh?'

They peered over to see if they knew us, gave a cursory wave and then turned away.

'Miserable sods!' Big Mick commented.

'Rob Parry reckons they're on the transfer list,' explained Mark

'So wha? They still owe it t' the fans,' Little Mick's sharp face matched his cutting remark.

The pub was full to bursting and Little Mick was voted to get the round in, as he could best squeeze his way through. Everyone was Cardiff. We, like many others, had to stand outside in the street. Mark sized it up for his 'On The Road' series in the 'zine. Paul was more loquacious now, saying things like 'Der, there's loads!' Big Mick seemed to know everyone. They gathered round him as if he were handing out fivers.

I was well gone. The pavement began to lurch. The sun and hoppy ale made me ridiculously optimistic. Steve Jones would be the new Mike England and nippy striker Jon Williamson would come off the list and prove to be a second Tony Evans. Nostalgia was a heavy brew.

I was slammed gutterwards by the arrival of the local constabulary. Their van screeching to a halt, as though they were about to raid the place. They approached groups of fans, including us, menacing like dogs whose territory had been taken.

'Get inside! You can't stand out here!'

'Look, there's no room! Wha 're we s'psed t' do . . .'

Mark's protest was cut short, as another PC grabbed hold of his pint and poured it down the drain. I could see Big Mick edging towards the conflict. Little Mick scowled and even Paul tutted. I could see it all 'goin off' in a second, when a flat-capped Inspector intervened, his palms opening and kneading air. He'd obviously been on a recent management course.

'Look boys, we don't want any trouble. There's a perfectly decent pub round the corner. Why don't you all go there.'

Big Mick seemed to inflate to the size of a barrage balloon. Then the air went out of him and he downed his pint in one gulp. It was a message to the rest. As we marched off we whistled the Laurel and Hardy theme tune. I'd never understood why it was designed to provoke the cops.

The next pub contained locals, who sought refuge in the lounge. After two rapid pints of a particularly punchy bitter which went by some ludicrous name like Natterjack, we made our weaving way to the ground, which had the absurd name of London Road (and we were in Devon!) It was a dilapidated affair, like a converted warehouse. We were perched on an open terrace, dazzled by the sunlight. Even in my drunken blur, I noticed how quite a few of our fans were unfamiliar. Some even spoke in Midlands accents! I was beginning to think we'd wandered to the wrong ground by accident.

When Tormouth came on, the abuse began.

'Freeman! You bent black bastard!'

'You poof Freeman! You shirt-lifting fucker!'

It started with individual insults and quickly developed into a chant among a small section of fans.

'He's a black arse-bandit! A black arse-bandit! Free-man! Free-man!'

'Bloody ell! Where 're they at?' I muttered to Little Mick.

This was not Cardiff. Apart from a few individuals, we weren't racist. I was totally sickened and shocked. I was ashamed to be wearing the colours. I focussed (as best I could) on Freeman from the kick-off. He ignored every single taunt.

It all came surging back, like rushing fans anxious to see. A fine prospect fallen on hard times, in footie cliché. The first footballer to 'come out'. A million pounder who hadn't quite made it. Two Barnardo's Boys, two adopted brothers.

For the first and last time, I literally willed an opponent to score against the team I'd followed since a boy. The more our clogging defender Jones lunged and swung at Freeman, the more Parry bit at his ankles, the more I wanted him to prove his point to all those bitter, bigoted minds.

Big Mick had deserted us for another group of fans. Mark yelled at our team like an irate trainer. Paul looked strained, as if holding back sympathy and only Little Mick shared my rage.

'It's so fuckin ignorant! Most of 'em 're problee BNP . . . I don' even recognise arf of 'em.'

'It's an insult t' true City fans,' Mick agreed.

When Freeman rose to a cross like a huge black bird rising then swooping down, I felt somehow responsible. Or was that just a ploy to assuage my guilt? When he scored what turned out to be the winner, I had never before experienced a silence like it. As he stabbed the air with a defiant fist like some

94

Black Power salute, all the abuse ceased, those callous gibes were mice scurrying for cover.

Shortly after, our clumsy giant Jones was sent off for hacking Freeman to the floor. They cursed his concrete boots and I noted a wry smile on Freeman's lips.

Leaving the ground, I was painfully cheerful in defeat. It was a strange sensation, like enjoying a holiday always aware of its end.

In the car home, I tried to instigate a debate.

'There woz racists there . . . there woz fascists tryin t' stir thin's up.'

'I think the bloke's fuckin brave, t' be onest,' added Little Mick.

Big Mick was unusually quiet. I began to wonder who his friends had been on the terraces. Paul had returned to his normal spot on the touchline. Only Mark dissented.

'Orright, fair enough, but ee musta known when ee come out. Ee woz bound t' get stick!'

'Oh, s' yew're agreein with all those prejudiced bastards,'re yew?'

'No, but . . .'

Mark's words trailed off the field of argument, to be replaced by familiar moans about our team and its future.

I wrote a scathing attack on the homophobia of some of our fans and sent it, as ever, to Little Mick for the fanzine. On the way down to Halifax at home, we picked up the 'zines from his house.

'Nice stuff, Wyn-o!' Mick enthused, but as I searched the 'zine I could find no trace of the article.

There was only Mark's account of the Tormouth match, with a fleeting mention of the Freeman goal and praise for Parry's single-footed defence. For me, that was the end of *Fly Bluebirds Fly*! I didn't even want to know Mick's excuse for not publishing. I could support Cardiff City forever, but the spirit of the 'zine had died.

Jason Freeman: his suicide, his last act of fame. But I'll always recall that bright yellow day of booze and vicious chanting. A day when loyalty and belonging was abandoned. I'll always recall his ecstatic expression after scoring and proud look of disdain at those who'd tried to destroy him, which cried out 'Insult me *now*!' Above all, I'll recall that silence which followed, like a minute in homage to a dead hero.

Avin a Field Day

Leap outa bed t' the piercin alarm. Sat'rday. Special. Tracksuit folded up waitin f' me. Course I ave to ang on till my ard-on goes down. Sundays is toss-up, reg'lar as chapel ewsed t' be. When -a 'Sunday Sport' come, need the stimulation, though it is gettin borin. Lemi Jerkov, Russian footballer: tidy joke, eh Micky?

Open-a bedroom door left-anded – very important – an 'en ave a cold shower. If we lose I musta missed summin. We win easy, I got t' work out what else I done. Even the order o' soapin as t' be right, leave the pubes till las thing.

On-a radio, talk of George Graham turnin Spurs round agen. All-a great managers got that motivation. Cloughie could make an average player into a really good un. I mull over ower new formation: free man an a marker t' watch Penôl's danger-man. 'Abercraig Boys' Club under 14's achieve the double under the managership of Micky Foley!' I cun see the local rag with a photo of me an-a boyz, sponsored by Phillips Pies. Oo ate em all? Looks like me.

My big poster ready with all the positions an arrows on. Coulda done a Don Revie, kept em in-a club'ouse overnight, stopped em drinkin lager and wankin too much. Or in Craig's case, a lot worse than tha.

The missis ud see the eadlines an larf, mockin my

love of the game, like she always done. Not at first though. Even brung er t' Cwmtaff Utd once, when we wuz courtin an she'd do ev'rthin to impress.

'Why 're them players wearin different colour shirts on, Micky?'

'They're the keepers, love. They ave t' wear different colours to avoid confusion.'

'An what about tha bloke in-a black? Ee aven touched-a ball yet.'

Tha woz the first an las time. Years arfta she become real cruel.

'All's yew go on about is tha Craig Bowen. Why don' yew go an live with im an is soccer-mad mam, Micky Foley, an give my ead peace? It's no fun bein a soccer widow!'

An worse still . . .

'The on'y balls yew got 're them ones in-a boot.'

But sex adn bin the problem. No, it wozn that, it woz ev'rythin else. Ev'ry little thin she done I couldn stand, an vice versa.

I struggle inta my tracksuit, my gut angin out like a floppy cushion. Since she gone, too much boozin, reg'lar rat-arse merchant. Now Craig's got a body on im. Not an ounce too much, all wiry. No doubt whatever, ee's summin else. Cun play anywhere, score from all angles, tackle, pass an beat players like they woz invisible.

My ard's gone down. The freezin water I spect. Jest think o' Craig's mam Dil an tha's enough t' make it flop. Dil's a Fanatic with a capital 'F', but also a right cow. Thinkin o' cows, I wonder if the missis ave done em? On'y f' little Alan o' course.

Ave my breakfast standin up, three shakes o' Krispies. Make my cup of Instant, take one sip an pour the rest down-a sink. Summin I definitlee forgot: but what?

Alan, named arfta Gilzean. My missis even gone along with tha then. Amazin! Now I'm bald as ee woz, but little Alan's got 'bout 's much skill as a corner-flag. In'erited Barbara's sportin talents, but I ave to play im. Does manage t' get in-a way sometimes. Know what Dilys thinks o' my selection. Yeard er stirrin, but she didn see the rest of it, did she? Along with Alan I brung is mates Kyle and Titch, super-talented players. Conveniently, she forget 'bout that.

As I get in-a car I rack my brains. Too late now anyway. Problee summin like pissin on-a bog-seat.

Fuck it! All tha worryin I take the wrong route. Easy as shit nowadays, with ower bran'new road system. More like a snakes 'n' ladders game. At Barb's new ouse in Beacon Villas I stop an beep the orn.

'Da da-da-da-da, da da!'

Could yer er in my ead – 'Micky Foley, predictable as the days o' the week! Alan! Urry up!'

'Oh mam, do I afto?'

Stuck onto a computer screen.

Ee slumps out carryin bags under is eyes, but no kit in sight.

'Alan! Don' forget the kit!' I shout. Ee stares blank.

'Don' know if mam's done it.'

'Whaaat?'

99

Control yewrself Micky. Ee's yewer's f' the weekend. Don' do a Strachan, worse still a Jock Stein. Sick that!

10 minutes t' meetin-up time. Alan fartin around as usual. Eventually ee collapses in-a front seat.

'Orright, son? All ready f' Penôl? Gonna stuff em, eh?'

Ee perks up sudden. I'm delighted.

'Dad?'

'Aye?'

'Okay if I go down town with-a boyz arfta the game?'

Ee don' give a shit. If ee wern my son I'd send im to a re-hab clinic f' computer addicts.

We arrive at-a club'ouse on time. On'y an an'full there, includin Dil standin like a statue, full of it. Plans f'r im t' day, yewr darlin Craig. First arf tha's all, see ow it goes. Chunky an Kev come over, often sub's, tryin to crawl.

'Micky! We ome or away?'

'Chunk! We're away, tha's why we're yer so early, see.'

'Micky, am I playin or wha? Speedy says las night ee int comin any more. Says ee's goin t' Morgantown.'

'Kev, tha's jest a malicious rumour spread by the tabloids.'

'Uh?'

Both boyz go off, gapin at my long words. I love takin-a piss, but cun see Dil means business, so I stride over to er, feelin er eyes go through me.

'Mornin, Mrs Bowen! Speed . . . er, Craig on is way, is ee?'

'Aye, ee will be 'less we start winnin. Morgantown ave bin arfta im, yew know.'

'I know, it woz on-a teletext,' I mumble.

'Pardon?'

'I know, it's jest a test. They're tryin t' disrupt ower plans. It's early season yet, Dil. Good win at Penôl an we're up there with-a big uns.'

I walk off with er words pursuin, 'Yew'll be lucky if ee comes t' day.'

'Smore 'an I'm likely t' do,' I wanna say.

I go round t' tick off those present. Alan's managed t' bugger off orreado with Titch an Kyle. Arris is busy showin why ee shouldn play in goals by doin kick-ups.

'Oo's in goals, Micky?' Is blonde bob stoppin f'ra second.

'Yew! Oo else?'

'No way! What about Rye?'

'Ee never turns up. Yew know as well as I do ee wuz grounded f'r about six years arfta knockin off the whool village's water supply.'

'Ee've bin suspended from school.'

'See what I mean. Totally unreliable. We'd ave more chance with Stan Collymore.'

'Ave we signed im, Micky?'

Arris: keeper, defender, great rugby-player by all counts. Thick as goalmouth mud.

It begins t' drizzle an gets eavier.

'Call on im, Micky. Ee wan's t' play. Tol me las night down-a Youth.'

'Till ee got banned from there.'

'Ow did yew know?'

101

Pissin rain favours Penôl. Slide tackles an dubious decisions. Three cars an luckily one belongs t' Kyle's dad, even though Kyle'll come with us. Councillor Evans t' be exact. People carrier. Bought on is expenses no doubt. Influence. Don' say a word.

In dribs an drabs 'ey all turn up, Speedy lookin glazed an is mate Fishy, super-skilled but don' get stuck in. Arris sticks is ead under my black 'n' white brolly.

'I int playin in goals, Micky. If I play in goals I'm gonna blow it!'

Before the game, doin a Ronaldo, eh?

'Orright, I'll call for bloody Rye. But if ee int ready yew play, okay?'

'Deal!'

Jumped up little prima-fuckin-donna!

'Get in-a cars, boyz! Wagons roll!' I announce.

Alan in-a back nex t' Titch an Kyle. Smell o' fags. Back of-a club'ouse problee.

'Boyz, yew bin smokin?'

'No, Mr Foley, onest!' Titch lies, grinnin. Titch still small, unlike Chunky oo's lost all is puppy fat.

I veer off toward Rye's an up the ill. The convoy follows. Rain tampin down now. Pitch-inspection weather. I know Rye's well from previous wakin visits. Good keeper, dependin on is moods.

I ammer is door t' no reply. See Dil gettin frustrated an Coun. Evans raise is eyes. Light on upstairs an Rye pokes is ead through-a window, yawnin.

'Oh hiya, Mr Foley. Wha's up?'

'Not yew Rye obviously! We gotta game against

Penôl. Yew playin or wha? Be ready in five, or we're off.'

'Aye, okay,' ee stretches. Doin us a favour.

I get ower kitbag outa boot an give it t' Bob Evans. Keep Dil out of it.

'Yew an Dil go a'ead. I'll catch up.'

Back in-a car I wonder why I bother. Alan echoes my thoughts.

'Don know why yew chase arfter im, dad. Arris is ower bes' keeper anyway.'

Summin lands on the roof with 'n ewge thud.

'Fuckin ell, what woz that? . . . sorry 'bout my language, boyz.'

I open the door t' see Rye racin from-a back of is ouse, grabbin is bag from my roof an jumpin in-a front, like the cops woz arfter im.

'Quick, Mr Foley, put y' foot down!'

I jest manage t' accelerate as is step-dad comes out in is vest mouthin off.

'Any good at lip-readin, Ryan?'

Ee takes a packet o' mingin Munchies from is pocket an lays inta them.

'I'm not shewer I should be bringin yew at all, y'know.'

'Sokay, Mr Foley. Ee's a wanker!'

'Oh, tha's orright then.'

As I bomb up-a sliproad, I rehearse my plan: 'Speedy, this is a special role f' yew. I know yew cun do it. Yew'll mark theyr bes' player Darren Davies. Yew know im from-a Cwmtaff team. That'll release Fishy f'ra free role be'ind the front two. So we'll be playin 3-4-1-2. Okay? Any stewpid questions? . . . Yes, Arris?'

'What about the keeper, or 're we playin three of em?'

'Orright, jest f' yew . . . 1-3-4-1-2 . . . Yes, Craig?'

'Bollocks, Micky!'

Rye lickin is fingers arfta mobile breakfast, Alan an Titch exchangin thoughts on best computer games, Kyle quiet as ever. Unlike is dad, chopsy bugger. Excellent left-winger, unlike is dad. Labour. All the bloody same nowadays. Concentrate on the game. Penôl pitch in view, don' look too bard t' me.

Bob Evans chattin up Arris's mam, mysteriously appeared. Proper blonde bomber. Down inta changin rooms. Pitch bein inspected by theyr manager, also ref mos' likely. Dil blockin the way, dead mean expression.

'Mr Foley, I gave the kit to Craig. There's all ell in there. Yew'd better sort it out.'

Kick open the door an dump the bag o' balls on top o' my folded master-plan. Scene of absolute bloody may'em.

'Sit down! Shut up! What the f . . !'

Speedy struttin the cat-walk of-a bench wearin a bra over is sweat-shirt, Chunky with knickers on is ead swingin on a peg, Arris twirlin another bra like a sling an Jordan West sniffin a nightie like some perve.

I reconize the nightie! Kit-bag empty. Not a shirt, sock or shorts in sight.

'Put em back in-a bag straight away!'

'Nice one, Micky,' sarks Speedy, as ee dumps the bra.

104

Glance at my watch. 10 minutes t' kick off.

'They belong t' yew, Micky?'

'No, Kevin, they're my wife's. She's avin a little joke I think.'

'Don' be s' darft, dad, it woz a mistake!' sayz Alan.

'Well, what d' yew know about it?' I turn on im, losin it f'ra second. 'Right, Titch, yew're captain. Yew tell Paul Williams, theyr manager, I'll on'y be 10 minutes an I'm sorry. Got it? Tell im it's not my fault.' Glarin at Alan.

'I should be cap. I'm the on'y Cwmtaff player, in I?' Speedy mutters to Fishy.

Fuck it, neally forgot! I touch-a changin-room floor an wipe both ands in sweaty dirt. So far no good though. Grab-a kitbag with as much of er stuff as I cun muster. Brush past an agitated Dilys oo peers down at its spillin contents – 'Micky, wha's goin . . .'

Drive back t' my missis' place like a nutter. On the way crayzee eadlines bug me like 'Team of Transvestites Trounce Penôl!' and 'Pervert Trainer Forces Boys To Play In Knickers!' The *Cwm Courier* ud ave a field day.

Dash up to er door, sweatin an puffin, my eart ready t' clap out. Ring. No answer. Push it. Bloody typical. Open.

'Barbara, the kit! Where is it? I need it quick! The match is startin! Barbara!'

Room t' room like a dog sniffin. Slow down, Micky, yew really will do a Jock Stein. Up-a stairs slow motion, like action replay.

'Barb! This is urgent!'

105

Swing open bedroom door. Barbara's ead peekin out from sheets. Some twat on top of er. Ee rolls off. Barb stops im from gettin outa bed.

'Oo the fuck?'

'It's on'y my ex. Ee's orright, Nev.'

Nev? Oo is it, Southall or wha? Cept ee looks thin with no mush an scared, would yew believe?

'Barbara, I need ower kit rapid! Where is it? I gotta a bag full o' yewer washin yer.'

I tip the contents on-a floor. She int impressed at all.

'Huh, football,' she smirks, 'mighta known . . . Jest get outa my bedroom an wait downstairs, I'll sort it in two ticks. Alan musta emptied the wrong bag. Blame yewr dozy son, Micky Foley.'

I leave Nev t' ide is passion. Shit, I even feel a stirrin myself. Not f'r er, but the scene. Feel like some smutty reporter, gettin in on-a climax.

Nex thing she's taken a bag an filled it with ower togs.

'Don' yew believe in knockin? I s'pose yew think it's funny interruptin like tha?'

I cun smell er, strongly moist as she bends over. My watch says arf-past. We could be docked points.

'Yew could've checked.'

'Ee dozn even want t' play f' yewr crappy team.'

'Go back t' Nev an collect yewr earnin's!'

'Fuck off, Micky!'

'Charmin!'

I afto ave the las word, even though she slams the door like a gun-shot. Arin back up Penôl. From-a road I cun see some match as begun! Penôl in familiar green an another team in pukey yellow. It's my team! It's Abercraig Under-14's without theyr trusted manager, oo've got the team-sheet, oo never done is pre-match talk an reg'lar warm-ups.

I steam through-a soddin rain an splash over t' Dil on-a touchline, jest as Titch beats theyr defenders to a long ball an, eadin f' goal, is whistled offside.

'Titch! Sort it out, will yew!' she yells, even though the ref's got it wrong.

Alan, one of the subs, trots up t' me lookin totally pissed off.

'Dilys, wha's goin on? The shirts!'

'Sorry, Micky. We ad to kick-off. Williams woz threatnin t' call it off an report us t' the league. We ad theyr trainin shirts.'

I cun see it's the best team an Dil's in er element, shoutin praise, slaggin off the referee. I ug the line nex to Alan oo bleats about bein cold an wraps is arms round isself. Serves im right. If she wern so uppity, I could fancy Dil. If she wern so married an all. Still, it 's a bloody conspiracy. Women takin over ev'rywhere arfta Thatcher. Gabby Yorath, Karen Brady, on'y a matter o' time before some Premier manager . . . Then Speedy scores a real cracker from outside the area. Dil leaps in the air an fists igh. Even Paul Williams carn disallow tha one. I smile at Dil an try t' seem appy. Nobody gives a toss about theyr star player.

'Dad! I'm gonna sit in the car. She won' bring me on! Gimme the keys.'

'Alan, I'm manager. I decide!'

Ee stares at me curious, sif I'm seriously lackin.

Eadlines zoom up at me – 'Dilys Bowen, First Woman Manager, Brings The Title Home!'

'Craig! Yew gotta watch theyr Number 10!' I belt out at Speedy, oo totally ignores me an roams, avin a field day.

The Davies Gang

Wha a larf! Me, live on telly! But I couldn smile even then. Never ave bin able to. Musta bin ammered inta me by the ol man. Wayne coulda done it great, o' course. Yew just ad t' look at im t' crease up in them days at school.

Goin live! I coulda looked straight at em friggin cameras an slagged em all off, them bastards oo laid inta us. My so-called father, oo never give a toss, among em. Why did ee ever ave kids at all, tha's what I'd like t' know?

But I didn. An I didn stammer neither, though my eart wuz beatin like a copper wantin to get in an search a place over. I jes tol em calmly bout me: tha special school in Bridgend where they showed me ow t' old a pen with pride. Prince Charles's scheme. Meetin im an them kids oo woz doin it an all. My stories an poems I wrote fer people on the 'state. Writin fer the baby in the womb, fer my friend's weddin. Whatever . . . I ad a go at it.

My brothers in jail, both of em. Ow I coulda gone the same way on'y . . .

An tha's all my dad yeard of the whool interview: Chris 'n' Wayne. Chris 'n' Wayne.

Ow could yew? Oo d' yew think yew are? Some kinda fuckin star?

I think ee wuz jealous, y' know. Ee'd like to ave

bin there, talkin bout is bloody opera records, is attic full of em.

Bet they ate me now. Most prob they seen it in Portland an in Swonzee.

Look at im, Carl Davies, my bro', mouthin off on- a box like some fuckin politician! Oo do ee think ee is anyway?

An Chris, it coulda bin yew. Yew ram yerself so fulla crap, yew ardly know night from day. An Wayne, yew coulda bin a stand-up comic, no problem. Made Owen Coyne seem like a lump o' lead with is pathetic jokes bout chinkies an spew.

Wha did we do, boys? We worked like a team, a famlee gang. We wuz the Crays up 'n' comin, the 'state's James gang. We slashed tha wanker's tyres coz them teachers wuz always pickin on us. Oh aye! So wha a great act it woz! I wish I'd given that school a bloody chance now. I wuz wild. They couldn tell me nothin an a belt round-a ead on'y made me crazier inside.

I climbed. 'Member boys? I scaled em wall-bars like bloody Spiderman an registration woz gymnastics over-a desk. I couldn stand a second my body wern doin summin t' get my juices goin. Even the coppers couldn reach me once. They chased me an I monkeyed up one of them tall lamp-posts along-a new road.

Come down, Davies! Jump!

They'd 've bin appy t' see me in pieces over-a pavement. The fuckers ad t'starve me down!

Now yer I am on crutches. Pride comes before a slide. Wanted to impress er kid, see? So I says, 'Look at me, Jason!' There I goes, arse over tit, the great

110

never-ave-been gymnast breakin my leg on ice. Jason woz really appy. Ee pissed isself an so did Julie, till I never got up. She's pregnant an ad a job liftin me, so's I thought she wuz goin t' ave a miscarriage on-a spot. Lovely place f'one, the ill down t' the Blue Pool an an even better one f'crackin yewr leg in arf. From Prince Charles Award t' Prince Charles ospital! Surprised I didn end up in-a new Maternity Ward!

Wayne! 'member the milk, mun? Tha wuz one of-a best yet. Should've got 'n enterprise award f' that. Spotted a demand, din we, eh? Trailin round them wards with all-a nicked bottles, supplementin theyr diet o' lumpy mash an runny jelly.

Think I'm gunna get pissed. Get tanked up an when I do anythin cun appen!

Anythin did appen!

I collected em round me, don' ask me ow! It wuz like 'ey wuz pushin me on. Great fuckin celebrity . . . I thought I'd show em!

Pint arfta pint arfta pint. Legless an mindless an ready t' join my two . . . Glass wern nothin.

'Go on Carl boy! Fer ol time's sake! Put-a boot in!'

An tha bloody plaster which had weighed me down like a ball 'n' chain become the ideal glass-breaker. Usin resources at and, eh Chris? Yew wuz always-a one with-a brains. The things yew could do with-a single screwdriver! Everythin cept openin up yewr own ead. Yew cun do tha with-a needle now, is it?

So I jes put my foot through an they all dived in, vulturin-a shop window. I didn get nothin. I done it

111

f' yew two, see? Couldn stand bein such a mammy's boy!

Mam! I'm sorry! Yewr the on'y one oo gives a damn bout me. I know tha. I'm finished with all tha. I'm on-a right track from now on. They jes disrailed me, them boys. I ad t' bust up all tha telly crap inta shards o' glass.

I know mam, yew never understood. Yew've struggled all yewr life on ands 'n' knees scrubbin-a floors fer-a pittance.

I tol em, the pigs. I stood up igh fer all of us. Leave off my brothers!

'Oh, so yewer the one on telly? Call this goin straight, sonny?'

I spat it all out at em from across tha table, mam. There wuz no way they were gunna slag off Chris an Wayne. Oo d' yew think yew are, yew fuckin pig bastards!

'Yew'll see them soon enough, Davies boy!'

Mam! I wrote a poem fer-a baby in Julie's womb. I know yew'd like it even if some of-a words ud sound strange. I'll write stories fer the baby an Jason when theyr older. They'll be presents like no others. Julie's lovely, mam, but she'll never ave me. She don' trust no-one. She've been beat up bardly by er ex, see. Oo cun blame er?

I know yew care, but yew never bothered neither. I coulda killed some copper an all's yew'd 've said woz 'Tha's orright, son!' If yew'd cared enough, yew'd 've come t' court with me. Ee's the other extreme, in ee,

112

the ol man! Is idea of-a tellin off is a quick kick in-a groin!

'Craig, yew silly fucker! Fancy lettin em catch yew! An yew didn even nick sod all, yew dull twat!'

Boys! Lookin back, we wuz a legend! But like all legends the endin's are tragic. Chris full of oles, like Bonnie an Clyde. Wayne tryin t' cut yerself up . . . oo wuz tha comic? . . . oh aye, Tony Ancock.

Nobody'll write bout us though. Nobody'll make films. An it won' be me, coz I wanna get away from it, see? Like-a distance between a boggin estate with its packs o' mangy strays an-a streams an trees of-a Beacons. I wanna catch autumn leaves fallin an write down theyr colours so's they don' blow away.

If I sound like a fuckin poofter, well too bard I say. Coz where's it all got us, eh? All-a friggin eadlines? We never done nothin worth a penny!

Me an Wayne nickin tha JCB an eadin fer Swonzee, when Chris wuz in there fer-a first time. The on'y criminals t' try an break inta a prison! An gettin inta Social Services t' find out what ower files said. When they tried t' take Chris away inta Care on is own, we sat on-a road in front o' tha car, din we?

When I think back on them things now, I think, Wayne, those 're yewr stories. What yew coulda done with them, standin in front of-a microphone don' bear imaginin! Mine 're all bout animals an rainbow bridges an tunnels inta the mountain with magic creatures at the end. Sounds like I'm trippin, but I'm not on-a magies.

113

I'd break my arm an all, t'get a larf out-a Jason. I'd write bout love in my own blood f' Julie. I'd do a lullaby yew'd call soppy t' welcome er ome with er little one.

But I'm not goin down. I'm not grabbin old of wha int mine no more. Coz even if it's-a on'y way out of-a grime, I'd sooner ewse my pen an-a rickety ol typewriter I picked up at-a local Jumble.

Boys! I'm not puttin yew down. Yew should take back what yewr deservin an I don' mean wha yew'd call ower share, coz tha's all in-a posh ouses by-a river. I mean-a wasted years, before yewr brain-cells 're turned inta mulch like piled leaves, Chris, an before there's no joke worth tellin when yew've strangled yerself, Wayne.

Hey, c'mon! The Davies Brothers! We could do it all different! Do it agen!

Novelties

I'm fed up of-a boredom. Yer I am perched like a pigeon, cept if I'd bin one ee mightn't 've left, coz ee spent all is time up in em lofts. An I wuz is omer, always returnin whatever. She's is tumbler, is bit o' fluff, is fancy woman. Performin all kinds o' tricks t' please im.

I ewsed t' love this view cross-a narrow valley, shakin ands with-a Aberbeeg Road, them neat little lofts b' there like tiny ouses. The bracken curlin in autumn like Nature's perm. Now, I ate it all! It's a bloody armpit an a man's one at that! It reeks o' stale booze, it's a loada tufts between slopes tha ardly let in-a sky. The road's so twisted down towards Cwm, it's like one of em metal puzzles I do put in sometimes. The on'y new thing appenin up yer is roadworks. Look at them trees, so forlorn. I know it's coz of the time o' year, but yew'd think they wuz dead if yew didn know better.

The on'y bits I d' like, is them two crops o' rock. They remind me of ol Westerns, cliffs stickin outa deserts. If I could get away, I'd take them with me! What a darft thought . . . 'Got anything to declare?' . . . 'Aye, two dirty great big lumps o' rock.'

Oh well, back t' bloody work. Snap, twist, lick. Drivin me crackers! Jes the sort o' joke . . . Tha's me, bit o' silvery paper. I still got it, but oo wants a

115

woman o' thirty-odd with a couple o' kids? Might as well be a prisoner. I 'member seein tha jail in Swonzee, thinkin o' prisoners lookin out t' sea with ev'ry wave repeatin 'Free, free'. A lot of cack on-a beach there they say. Mind, I'd still like t' live overlookin-a Bay, with tidy shops nearby. All we got round yer is-a Spar.

A joke, a ring. I don' wear it no more. Not tha ee'd notice if ee wuz still yer. 'What d'yew call a man oo fancies pigeons? . . .' 'A pervert!' With this ring, I thee name. Ne mind, tonight's the night . . . Trish . . . she's orright an er usband's great. I even seen im doin-a ironin! Now Chris woulda called im a 'bender', but ee's almost tha New Page man. Course, ee d' get jealous, mind, an Trish as t' be in when ee says. But at least she gets out now an agen.

Put on yer paper at, we're goin t' ave a party! I'm gunna look real sexy . . . tight skirt an silky white blouse. Do my face up tidy. Six lagers an I'll be flyin igh. Won' feel like comin ome at all. A big man from somewhere foreign. Jamaica or summin . . . passin through with is reggae band. Or Cardiff even . . . 'Why don't you come for a drive in my car, young woo-man?' . . . The way ee'd say it, real slow, enough t' make yewr juices flow . . . 'I know jes the spot. Beyond Trefil . . . there's a disewsed quarry . . . I ewsed t' do my courtin . . .'

My ands achin like I've got arthritis orready. Bent over this table. I'm sick of it! It's time I got-a kids . . . 'Mam! Mam! Cun we pull one?'

Tha's one thing I'm not goin t' buy this Christmas. We'll make ower own. It's easy kids. On'y we'll do it tidy, not like these yer rip-off things. We'll ave real magic fish inside tha glow an go all colours accordin t' wha yewr future's goin t' be. My fish'll go green. What'll tha mean? Sickness or a change o' scene?

'Leave them bloody crackers alone, will yew? I tol yew before! Bloody ell they get ev'rywhere! . . . If I lose them, I lose money an bloody Santa don' come coz I gotta pay fer im same as evry'thin.'

An Darren looks at me all knowin an says, 'As Santa got bailiffs too, Mam?' Der, tha boy's got 'n ead on im fit f' Mastermind! Don' know where ee d' get it from. Not from me. Words never bin my strong point.

Out on-a town, gettin it down. Kids dumped on my mam. Jes fer once, mam love. It's on'y me an Trish. No arm.

'Ow's trade, Deb?'

'Wish I wuz goin t' be pulled like them flamin crackers, Trish!'

'Yew never know yewr luck!'

An we larf. If ower larfs ad wings they'd 've taken us t' Florida. Not tha I wanna go there. Mickey bloody Mouse? Too much like what I do fill em with.

Two young men on-a untin expedition. All glossy sportswear.

'Goin joggin, boys?'

'Either of yew from Jamaica?'

'Yew mus be pissed!'

Bonkin in-a disewsed quarry! Ow romantic! Back seat with furry covers (imitation, o' course!)

117

'Trish! Le's go up-a Club!'

She looks so funny when she's pissed. Er eyes d' pop outa er ead. Er face is like plasticene!

'The Club?'

'Yeah!'

'The Comrades?'

'Neow! Habergavenny Glof Club!'

I says, tryin t' talk real posh an gettin all-a words wrong, as usual.

'The on'y time a woman goes into the Comrades Club is t' clean-a bogs out, Trish. Are yew takin the piss?'

'I don' care! We'll show em!'

'Are yew prepared?'

'Ow d'yew mean? Ave I got a packet o' condoms?'

'Na! I mean ave yew got a machine-gun?'

The long road t' the Comrades. Chippie on-a way. Followed by-a two fitness freaks with-a spare bellies. Maybe I put too much scent on! I trip on-a step outa the chippie an one of em tries t' come to the rescue. Trish throws im a chip.

'Yer! Tha's the on'y bite yew'll ave tonight!'

As we larf agen an walk away they tell us t' 'Fuck off, yew slags!' an the Comrades come jest in time. They don' follow us in coz they think we're goin t' get ower ol men in there.

Me an Trish like two bloody Martians landin. Ower stockin'ed legs showin up like antennae. Them male ewmans gawpin. The silence before an explosion, an then . . . nothin nasty, but loads o' comments comin at us from all sides. Even-a barman says, 'Wha yew want, love? Or need I ask?'

118

'Is this really 1991?' Trish says, gettin stroppy, 'or ave we gone back a century?'

Oo should appear, comin from-a bogs, zippin up an burpin with all-a manners of a runaway juggernaut, but Chris!

'Bloody ell, Debbie! Wha yew playin at? Yew finally flipped, or wha?'

So I grab-a nearest pint an flung it in is gob!

'Tha's fer ol time's sake!'

We run out, gigglin like mad. Ower noise seems t' spin the town like one o' them ol-fashioned tops. The pavements wobble to a stop, so we run till we catch up with-a expression on is face. Stunned! It ud bin like I'd undressed im in front of the boys an made is willy shrink t' the size of a peanut.

We run in-a direction of Trish's ome. I'm drinkin the air an it tastes better 'n all them lagers.

Suddenly, Trish catches old o' my arm an pulls me to an abrupt alt.

'Deb! I thought I seen em boys!'

'So? Didn yew fancy em?'

'Don be darft, I'm a married woman!'

'So wha? This is ower fling, init?' An I flap frantic once agen, till I come to a ewge sign. It's brandnew an as the face of a clown on it. It says 'This way to 1992'.

I think I'm seein things, but Trish reads it out loud. Its arrow points towards a rough track which jes leads t' ol waste-tips. Although er ouse is nearby yer, I notice now tha Trish is shittin erself. She musta really seen them boys an thinks theyr followin us.

'Deb! Le's go up my ouse an ave a couple there, eh?'

I'm beyond though. My ead's still up above, circlin. 'C'mon. Don' be borin! This is the path to the future! Let's go an see what it brings!'

She squeezes my arm so tight it urts bard. She stares so ferocious, I think she's goin t' slam me one.

But I shake myself free an stumble up-a uneven track. All-a time I'm ascendin inta dark, I yer er shoutin while I keep goin up.

Steps be'ind me. Them boys agen! I run inta the night. It pulls me down with its weight. There int no future yer, the ground's broken, the track disappears! I cun yer my eart clear. Fer ev'ry beat there's a step. My ankle gives way, twists, I slide an tear my tights. Oh bugger! I feel-a skin scraped on my leg.

I lie listenin. Nothin cept-a sound o' car engines risin up-a valley-slopes like smoke. Maybe they've gone back, given up chasin. Woz tha sign theyr little trick, theyr joke t' lead us away?

But it int us, it's on'y me. I know ow them trees feel I cun see from my window. Might as well be them: fixed, lonely an waitin. Fer wha? Birdsong?

I'm bloody freezin! Put my ands in my coat-pockets. Oh no! I don believe it! Two crackers! The kids musta . . .

Le's ave a celebration, Deb. After all, this is 1992, almost a month before it's yer. What's goin t' come out? My wages? Now that ud be a real joke!

'Wha d' yew call a cracker-worker oo earns buggerall?'

'Desperate Debbie.'

So I take one end in one and an one in-a other an . . . phut! Like avin it off with Chris! Not with a

120

bang, but a wimp (I read tha once in school, I'm shewer). I wipes my leg with-a at. Where's-a toy? Bet there int one. Typical! Oo made this crap? . . . Oh aye, it were me!

No, there it is. Wha's tha? I don' member puttin tha in. A tiny Japanese pagoda. Ow useless cun yew get? I bury it in-a coal rubble an fist it down.

Well, le's try the other . . . Pull . . . Snap! Tha's a better one. Wha d'yew drink at a party on-a slag-heap?'

'Coca Coal-a!'

An-a toy this time's jest as weird. A train on-a bit o' string. I think tha cun join-a pagoda.

I'm knackered. I uddle up an don' care no more. Even Trish left me t' go ome t' er darlin an a cup o' cocoa. I dig my eels inta the loose surface like I'm tryin t' put my roots down. I close my eyes. I'm givin up flyin, coz in the end yew always land somewhere like this. Jes waste on-a waste dump. An I can't grow yer coz there's no soil an anyway, oo'd come t' look at me? The kids ud climb fer a short time, my mam ud water an care . . . I got this strange sensation o' them two novelties growin even outa this wilderness an then collapsin agen as if they'd never bin there. Next year I'll look this way an they'll be the size o' factrees. But fer all tha, they'll be balloons. Burst inta nothin.

My fingers feel fit f' breakin, like rotten twigs. I pick myself up an try t' stagger back. If this is next year, I won' be followin no signs in future. Wha wuz-a clown smilin bout? Sick, I reckon.

Even when I yer Trish's voice callin me from-a

distance, it don' make me feel no better. Seems like I bin away frages. I'm torn up an flung away, like them boys ud caught up an abused me. I goes blubberin inta Trish's arms like a baby.

'Deb, love! Wassa matter?'

She pats my back as though she woz windin me!

'Trish, I jest ad a funny experience with a train an a pagoda!'

'Yew mean yew jest ad too much lager!'

We giggle agen like a couple-a ens. Then we walks up er ouse arm in arm an er ol man gives er stick fer gettin back so late. I begin t' wonder if ee int like all-a rest of em.

Finally, I collapse on er sofa with-a las vision o' Chris's face soppin an drippin beer. I smile asleep like I never done before.

Lost Ighway

'I'm so lonesome I could cry.' Ank baby, 'ey don' lissen, do they? It's all self-pity, but when there's no one left t' pity yew, eh? I'm walkin away, Ank mun, I'm walkin away. Where to, I dunno. I'm on a lost ighway. I int the on'y one, but I got friends think they'd won-a lottery ev'ry week with money t' burn.

Smoke bilges down from-a fields o' bracken. Them bloody arse'olists at it agen. Summertime greys not blues I reckon. Shoulda bin born on top o' the mountain. That way I'd-a got work no problem. Different perspective see, lookin down on ev'ryone, 'stead o' crawlin along-a valley bottom like some slug, jest t' be crushed by a tire.

Lost ighway, road t' nowhere. Plenty t' do round yer they say. Aye, plenty t' do, but no fuckin work! Oo onestly cares till they get where I am t'day?

Leavin the village be'ind. Taddy's ouse and then Miffy's, where ee's problee umpin away upstairs by now. Is missis, she's gorgeous. Ow ee got er I carn say.

The smoke gets t' me. I cough like I'm gonna puke. Soon the whool illside'll be black. Soon we'll ave wooden windows f' ev'ry shop 'n' pub. But lovely roundabouts. Tha one a'ead's got *Croeso* in flowers an a rock garden fit f' ra mansion. We'll ave

123

roundabouts with fountains an benches, picnic places to admire ower posh road system.

They put it there coz of the factree. Now it jest goes round an round in endless circles like-a shows on Barry Islan'. I op on it, sit on a flat lump o' rock. It's spinnin as I lean back, gaze at-a sky. The letters of *Croeso* whir an blur below stars. The moon ides be'ind clouds, wishin it ud die.

'I'm so lonesome I could cry.'

I leap off, angin onto-a lamppost f' support. Ank! Brawd! Yew an me, eh? They never understood.

'Countree? They call it tha coz it's played by cunts! Yee hi!'

There's a sign, ewge an practiclee bran' new – SUNG PLANT. Well, if this is a fuckin plant it never even ad any roots, ne' mind growin. An then next to it, carn believe wha I'm seein. It says FOR SALE in big red letters, like it wuz an ouse or summin. Like some div businessman's gunna be passin by, spot it an say to issell 'Yes, think I'll purchase that factory to add to my collection. After all, it's awfully clean!'

I try my pockets. Not a pen in sight. I wanna write summin that matters, summin intelligent, but all I cun think of is stewpid jokes about singin which don' fit. For sale, ower future, gon t' the ighest bidder – a slaughter-ouse, another hyper-bloody-tension-market.

Up the windy drive where er Majestee once come to open it. The grass blades wave theyr banners. The stars are paparazzi. Whatever, I'm yer t' declare this factree officially empty. Not long it'll be full I yeard t'day. My own car a goner yesterday, too dear t'

124

repair. An wha do I yer down-a club? A second-and car showroom, tha's what! Prices beyond me.

I declare this plant dead in its pot. No, looks like it never bin ewsed. An tha's the secret. Ladies an gentlemen of the press, this woz the factree what never woz. It woz money, it woz bankruptcy and Sung (oo ever ee is) might as well've bin leader of-a Moonies.

The empty car-park. Factree buildin polished as a gun-barrel. Big letters o' SUNG like ower OLLYWOOD, one side of-a valley. An there it ends. This place mus' be cursed. Look at tha massive D scarred ond-a grass where ower ski-slope ewsed t' be?

Then tha line of em. JCB's what never got made yer, shipped in specially for Lizzie Windsor's benefit an left for God knows what. A row of fuckin toys, 'cept it int a game.

Go straight up t' the first, dyin f'ra burst. Take out my prick an anoint it. Cun yew imagine Prince Philip? My piss makes a pleasant stain. Dog nights. Ank, yew woz-a first rolling stone. The sin jest too much, there wuz a whool road made of it. My missis comin ome from-a supermarket.

'I bin lookin f'jobs love, onest. There int nothin. I'm too old, too expensive.'

My son lookin down on me. I carn face im no more. Ee've done so well, off t'uni. No trouble at all, not like them crazee kids angin around-a Square, inta drugs, booze an stealin. I know what ee's thinkin – 'Yew're a failure, dad! Mam's keepin yew an you still piss it all away down-a club, as if nothin mattered.'

125

Wish I ad a sandy, or even arf one. I'd smash ev'ry window of these JCBs. Jac Codi Baw: my daughter's book. Don' sound right t' me. More like 'Jack Cunt Bastard' I kick the tyres an clamber up t' the driver's compartment. No way in. Pull myself onta the roof, slippin and swearin.

Ank, yew save me agen boy, as I owl at-a sky, las' wolf of the Taff valley . . .

'Now I'm lost, too late t' pray.'

There's the new road opposite, goin past, goin away. Ower ouse down in-a village, the missis sleepin by now. Good woman oo don' deserve me. Nothin but a burden. But is it my fault, Ank, baby? Summin bout a world economy, the East goin down like-a Titanic? I should never ave taken it. Sposed t' be a new start. Ridin my ope. Now all's I'm ridin's this ewseless digger.

Tha roundabout's like a dartboard. Carn even do tha no more. My one chance of ittin the target. Ev'ryone down-a club said it. 'Al – yew're fuckin magic! Yew're a natural, no bullshit!' An I could do it, no matter wha . . . triple top . . . undred and eighty. Ad the eyes f'r it. Snake eyes like Dustin Offman in tha injun movie. My son Ioan got no time f'r it, calls it sad an ol marn gettin s' worked up bout these little arrows.

But t'night I blew it. We needed a double three t' win. Normlee no problem. It got t' me sudden. All I could yer wuz Ank singin. 'For a life of sin I've paid the cost.' Like someone ad turned on a juke-box in my brain. I blew it Big Time. I woz eyeing up, squinty, when my arm jes flopped. The darts fell from my ands onto the mat. I stood gawpin at-a board sif I'd seen my own ghost.

'Wha's up, Al? Yew orright?'

'C'mon mun, yew cun do it.'

Then I run. Down-a river first. Thinkin o' yew, Ank, o' nothin else. The river all dried up. Some woman leavin yew gaspin. Wen' down three times, come up twice. My missis at ome patiently waitin. There's the difference, eh? Me always avin a go at er, explodin bout small thin's. Yew could even drown yewrself in there.

So I end up yer, empty as the place isself.

'C'mon yew darft fucker!'

Kick my legs on 'is spankin bright dinosaur. It don' shift. No midnight train, on'y groanin traffic through still air.

'Yee hi!' I goes. 'Yee hi!' Takin-a piss outa pisstakers.

I dismount, slidin an tumblin. My bladder painin. I baptise another wheel, leavin my mark.

'You always were a prick, dad!'

Yer Ioan's voice mockin. Ee's right. The road down's rough, never smooth eh, Ank? Month I wuz born yew died. Eart attack they said. Like fuck it woz! An Endrix died o' food poisonin!

Bloody ell, they've turned 'is path into an escalator. I'm goin in-a wrong direction an all. Kerbs 're high as steps. Should be soberin up, but it's gettin worser. Problee all tha smoke. Wern from-a fire, but from marajoanna. Some'ow I make it t' the roundabout an collapse by-a flower-bed.

I pull myself up, determined t' do summin

worthwhile, t' make a real job o' this pointless sign. I yank up all-a flowers one by one an pile em at the centre. I take the CROESO apart an make a bullseye where I sit, appy in-a middle. I'll stay yer, who gives a shit? The missis'll die of embarrassment an Ioan'll find it funny.'

A police siren breaks inta the valley's silence like a burglar 'larm. About time. Them boyz've problee done a runner. Typical cops, always arrive when-a trouble's over.

Nex thing it stops, brakes screech an I see em. Torches shine straight in my face. Shoutin an abusin.

'Yer yew! What do yew think yew're doin?'

I get up, sober an shittin myself. Suddenly a middle-aged man on-a dole stuck in-a load of uprooted flowers.

'Bloody eck, Mark, it's a wrinkly vandal!'

'Ey – lesso' that!' I blurt, without thinkin.

They aul me to the Panda, bits o' petal an leaves still clingin. Don' ave no choice. Feel like pissin agen. Shrunk t' the size of a naughty schoolboy. Blabberin 'I never done nothin! Them flowers wuz there before I sat down! . . . what's all the fuss about?'

'The fuss is damagin public property. Anyway, yew were seen. We ad a report.'

'Aye, there's camras in Sung's. Yew'd be surprised, grandad.'

'It might've been im done them fires as well, Mark.'

They larf, jest like my son. Two young cops oo fling me in-a back o' theyr car, sif I'm a thief or murderer.

128

Camras, eh? CCTV t' protect buggerall.

Neither good nor bad, just a bit like you! I sing out loud.

'An we'll do yew f' noise pollution if yew don' shut it!'

Ank, yew suffered, I carn deny it. Forgotten, lonesome, singin countree, singing-a blues. Poor white trash, jest like me.

Some Kind o' Beginnin

The sound o' voices rises from-a street. More banterin 'an arguin, but it still brings back tha night. There's too many thin's remind me. Ev'ry time I see Dave on telly playin fer-a Jacks. Ev'ry time I go out to a Club (though tha int often nowadays) an there's a barney.

Puttin on my face, layer 'pon layer, I carn elp thinkin ow she must afta dollop it on t' cover over wha I done. An there by my mirror is-a cuttin. People might think I'm sick or summin, but I jus don' wanna forget. It's a warnin: NEVER AGEN!

Wish I wuz goin out with them girls. Theyr jokin pierces-a glass an ruffles-a curtains. A whool gang of em, I bet, like we woz in Merthyr, me, Nadine, Andrea an Jayne (with a 'y' don' forget, she'd say). I long fer theyr voices now, goin up an down like-a mountains an valleys. Funny tha', it's flatter down yer an-a way 'ey talk ave not got the same music to it some'ow.

Mascara, face cream . . . owever much I put on, I could never be like er. My teeth stick out in funny ways an I got ooded eye-lids like my dad wuz an owl or summin. I light up a fag an burn an ole jest above er ead. I 'member wha ee once said, 'Martine, I'm sorry t' tell yew, but yewr breath's mingin . . . Yew should try an give up.' But all em months in the Centre I needed em so much. I'll never stop now, not even if I seen im agen.

The thin's the papers said, an mostly true I know. But oo cun understand all 'at goadin? All 'at gangin up an pickin on me er friends done? It wuz like Cardiff 'gainst-a Jacks, we all knew it wuz gunna go off sometime, but no one spected I would make it appen.

I blow smoke at er picture. The eadlines blur. I yer my flat-mate Chrissie come in from work: tidy job in-a Travel Agents, all dolled up. She's like me, tryin t' make a new life. She've ad 'n ard time, brought up in-a Omes. Carn understand ow she's so straight-lined though. TV on, cuppa tea next . . .

'Hey, Martine! D'you want a cuppa?'

'No ta, Chrissie! I'm off soon!'

She knows all 'bout me, but it don't bother er. She reckons er dad done worse thin's than tha to er an er mam.

Tha bloody burn above er air looks like a friggin alo! I feel like ashin tha photo once an fer all, but instead I stub-a fag out on-a mirror, right where my teeth jut out comical.

Chrissie looks so relaxed in-a sittin room when I enter, feet up an sippin away. As she turns er head fer a moment she reminds me of er, tha beaky nose an pointy chin, but . . .

'Martine, you look great!' she says, an I do feel ready t' face the world, even though I wan' more.

'Aye, but oo cares in tha poncy otel?'

'Well, maybe you'll meet someone tonight. Some

131

millionaire soccer star'll be passing through and propose to you over his lasagne!'

'Soccer star?'

'Oh . . . sorry Martine!'

I larf an she wriggles in er chair an echoes me. Soon it's 'S'long!' and 'Bye.' Me wonderin ow she cun talk so posh with er background an ave survived.

The streets o' Abernedd turnin inta Merthyr by the second. Cack-jumpin an spottin where yesterday's shops ewsed t' be. See-through windows replaced by a environmentally-friendly sort, perfect fer graffiti an posterin. Local bands like Panic Stations an The Pocket Billiards advertisin gigs. I woz inta football when my friends listened t' the Merthyr equivalents o' them. I woz turned on when Merthyr played the Jacks (Dave wern with em 'en) an stood with Dazzy an the boys chantin an loathin to a pitch where I lost myself.

Wassa time? Shit! Four minutes late an moany ol cow Thorpe'll be bound t' dock me.

Car beeps me. Two boys in overalls, all over painty. Give em a V and see em mouthin off at me.

There it is at bloody last, The Dog and Duck, Abernedd's finest, 3 star, AA. Looks real tidy from-a front an all, but I could blow it open, wha with ol Thorpey an is stingy ways . . . scrapin-a mould off of fruit an tha ol can-opener sheddin rust!

'Yer! Wha's this in my peas, waitress?'

'Oh, I believe it's some sort o' garnish, sir.'

When in doubt, call it garnish, tha's wha ee tol us t'say.

Just as I'm gaspin fer a fag an fumblin in my pockets, Thorpey ops through-a door t' greet me.

'Martine, you're five minutes late again. It'll have to stop, Marteen!'

Sayin my name like I woz 'n alien. Feel sorry fer is missis, I do. Imagine im on top on the job . . . 'You've had your ten seconds heavy-petting, dear. Now we'd better hurry up and start breathing faster!'

'Marteen! Stop grinning and get ready, will you!'

Soon I'm all frilled up an layin-a tables, all-a time chattin t' Michelle oo on'y jes started las week an oo keeps cockin ev'rythin up. She's so nervous an tryin t' please, but Thorpey give er so much jip when she wrote-a orders down wrong, she nearly give up on er first day. An the bloke what ad steak 'n' kidney pie 'stead o' steak! I thought ee wuz gonna crack er one on-a spot!

Lee, the main chef, ee takes-a piss outa Mich no end. Ee tried it with me when I begun, so I tol Mich t' take no notice. But she don' know when ee's bullin or not. Ee tol er the correct way t' serve chips wuz with a fork an she believed im. By-a time she'd got em on-a plate, they'd frozen agen!

Friday evenin, but it's real quiet. I serve a family with a stroppy veggie wife an two kids insistin on avin adult portions.

'What's this Vegetable Steak Casserole?' she asks.

'Oh no,' I says, 'tha's vegetable casserole with steak in it.'

'But it does say Vegetable Steak, doesn't it?'

This coulda gone on forever, on'y er ol man tells er t'ave-a veggie lasagne.

133

Lee's outa is ead as per usual. I reckon ee's on summin, I do.

'One veggie lasagne, but I reckon there's some rat in it somewhere, Martine . . . Look! There's its brother!' ee yells, pointin is spatula at-a corner of-a kitchen. I twirl round like a ballerina, then give im a shove in is bulbous beer-gut an ee makes out t' swat me like a fly. Mich comes in lookin all excited like she seen some lush pop-star. She catches old o' my arm, while I'm on-a look-out fer ol Thorpey, oo always seems t' rush in when we int workin tidy.

'Martine! There's these really ace boys! . . . Yew gotta come an give me an and! I'm on pins!'

'Aye, I will, arfta I done this one table. Okay?'

So I takes in the veggie lasagne an the usband's ome made pie (what comes straight from-a freezer) an ave a gawk. There's a loada tables put together an, jest as Mich said, a pile o' stonkin men and boys in posh suits an flash ties. Then I see Thorpey chattin to an older man oo wuz with em an ee glares over at me, so I make out I'm busy servin the famlee.

As I'm dishin out-a veg, I yer a Merthyr voice an 'n unmistakable one at tha. I practically fling-a veg onto the bloke's lap an spatter im with gravy. The back end o' Dave's ead, I'm shewer.

'Excuse me!' says the bloke.

'Oh, I'm sorry!' I grovel, in case ee should call Thorpey. I do a rapid runner back to-a kitchen an grab old o' Mich, oo's gotta andfull o' prawn cocktails.

'Well, Martine, what d'yew think, eh?'

'Mich! Lissen! There's this boy I ewsed t' know

134

there . . . I think theyr Swonzee football team . . . I gotta do the next servin, right?'

Coz I'm so igh-pitched an wound up, Lee yers me over is sizzlin chip-oil an steak-bashin. Is face is a pumpkin grin.

'Ne mind the rat, where's the fuckin poison? I could never stick the Jacks!'

'Don' be darft, Lee. Ee's from Merthyr.'

'Ey, Mart, I thought yew were a true Bluebird.'

'Tha's all in-a past . . . Right, Mich, give us them prawn cocks!'

Michelle's nearly creamin er knicks on-a spot, she's so worked up.

'Ey, we could be on yer . . . I fancy the big black one, I do!'

'I gotta black puddin in the fridge, if yew don't get off with im,' shouts Lee.

'Shurrup Lee, y' racist dick!' I yell as Mr Thorpe comes bustin through-a door. Ee's tampin an is ard white face its me like a breeze-block.

'Martine,' ee whispers snakey, 'just get on with the job or you're out! Right?'

I feel like tellin im t' stuff it, but I iss back 'Yes Mr Thorpe!' I go calm but quick inta the dinin area an make a point o' servin Dave first. I glance over t' see Mich urryin towards the big black fella, oo looks real chuffed. Dave's busy talkin, so I lean right over im, cranin t' face im like I wuz goin t' give im a peck.

'Yewr prawn cocktail sir!' I says, so deliberate an sarky ee turns straight away, lookin curious till ee reconises me. Is eyes 'n mouth narrow t' three blades. Then ee turns away with a flick o' is ead like ee wuz eadin-a ball or summin.

As I return to-a kitchens I yer im callin me back. I don' wanna respond, but thinkin o' Thorpey's warnin, I decide to.

'Uh . . . scuse me, waitress, but can I ave my steak well done, please? I carn stand the sight o' blood!'

An all-a players larf, like it woz some private joke.

'Yes, of course sir!' I feel like spittin out-a words, but I control myself, savin it up. Inside, I'm so angry coz ee treated me like I woz nobody. All is indifference brings it back: ow ee ewsed me against er, er against me. I seen ow ee wanted us t' be total enemies. An I played is game orright . . . a Stanley knife I on'y brung fer protection . . . she wuz avin a go at me all-a time . . . 'Martine, yew've lost im, yew bitch! Le's face it, yewr a loser!' . . . Blood everywhere. Now I gotta remember. Er blood on my clothes an ands: I knew I'd never wash off them stains. An when Dave says bout is steak jes then it seemed aimed, like is sharp eyes shinin.

I decide t' take in these special steak knives we aven ewsed frages an Lee thinks I'm darft.

'Wha yew wanna bother with em for? I need em f' choppin up the rats anyway.'

'Lee do me favour an chop yewrself up, they'll be one less rat then.'

I rub my and cross-a blade o' one. I feel scared an thrilled at-a same time. Mich comes in grinnin all over er body, as if she've oready got tha fella. I old up-a knife towards er.

'Ey, Martine! Go easy! I never spoke to yewrs. Onest!'

'It's okay, Mich. This one's fer im!' I clatter-a knives onto a tray, leavin Michelle stunned.

This time I take it real slow, as if I woz strokin. I know wha I'm doin, so's I ask oo's avin steak an watch is face as I carefully place each knife. I old each one a while before puttin it down an I cun see is panic risin. Ee cun see I'm leavin im till last an ow much I'm relishin it all. Looks as if ee's shittin is load when I finally come t' im.

'Yew avin steak, sir . . . Well done, wern it?'

'Er . . . aye . . . ta.' Ee tries t' act so cool, but is ands 're fiddlin with is other cutlery, as if ee's searchin f' weapons!

I take old o' the las steak-knife an prepare t' show im. Now ee'll get the message. I cun take down tha cuttin. I cun wash off tha red. I sweep the knife up to is face an ee jerks back in is chair, nearly fallin. At-a same time, Michelle comes in screamin, 'Don' do it, Martine! Don' do it agen!'

An I says t' Dave, real calm . . . 'Is this done enough fer yew sir?'

Ever'thin appens so quick, I think I've sliced im without knowin. Is team-mates 're laughin, Michelle grabs my arm an Thorpey's fussin an pullin me back t' the kitchen. Ee drags me outa the door inta the yard. I still gotta knife, but there's no blood anywhere t' be seen.

'This is no joke, Martine! How dare you treat our customers like this? Who do you think you are? You can't . . .'

137

I fling the knife to the ground an-a sound severs is words, leaves em angin.

'Yew cun stick yewr bloody job, Mr Thorpe! I wozn messin, fer yewr information, it wuz fer real. I owed tha boy one!'

'I should never have taken you on . . . I knew about your record, you know . . . They told me you'd changed . . . Now, get out of my hotel!'

I undo-a apron an scrumple it up as ee shoves past me. I fling it in-a bin an feel a real buzz, though ee never seen me.

As I stride away down-a street, a coach passes an faces stare at me with a 'Wow' on theyr lips. All of em 'cept one, that is. I lost so much to im: my body, my freedom an now my job. I'll go ome an take-a scissors to er photo. Cut it up inta tiny pieces knowin tha won' be the end, but tha problee, this is some kind o' beginnin.

Sara's Story

At fourteen, strokes of rust in her hair, nose-ring bullish. Still dazzle-eyed and scratchy voice of a slow 45.

She read 'Goggle Eyes' and she was there. Her own fugitive father the one thing made her swear like back-seat boys.

She was a Zelig of the regions: from Scouse to Deep South, Russell to Angelou, she intoned, an actress of the lined room, her sounds making journeys she'd despair of ever . . .

Her mam came to gather up comments one evening. I saw pride as she soaked them in, smiles fluid.

It began. I never noted. Her pupils hardening to needle points. Her concentration all downward to a single graffitied name in felt. 'MIFFY' seemed so innocent, fluffy toy taken to bed. Till she said – 'I'll send him a poem in prison.'

Her creations weirdly different. Animals let out to roam from battery cages where they'd been fed the remains of kin. They hopped, stumbled, leapt over the page-lines.

She couldn't be confined. Down town once, she attacked the fresh air, kept jerking back to the pub's smokey door, mouthing into the afternoon quiet. Her voice had become cracked vinyl, a broken chorus.

Day after day, her empty place. I pleaded for somebody to read.

Heard her story only as she began to pull out: the baby and the smack, holes in her arm no words could fill. Her boyfriend the dealer, a hangman on every card.

Those animals had escaped so far she couldn't find them. I'd imagine her searching the Beacons, dark hair straggled, her player's tones calling for a script.

Remarkably, she returned, wheeling them all home to the estate. Each one to be nurtured. Each with its own distinct and gleaming accent.

Cellohead

'Cello'ead!' they called out, at the boy with a lump on his back. The case, the wooden body.

'Yew're a spoff!' at his wide-rimmed specs, the boy with bow growing from his right arm. Despite his left kicking foot, his forehand smash swing, they goaded him, drumming his hunch with 'Ey, Mo's Art! Poofter fuckin moo-sick!'

They'd pluck his strings like feathers of a hen. They'd turn his pegs till he was out of tune, tramp his bridge till it snapped. They'd tear out the hairs from his bow at the roots.

One school assembly he shut their taunts in his case, those stickers from Kernow, Alba, Éire, Breizh made them mute.

Fauré's *Elégie* and tears they couldn't swallow or hide. Even the most solid pupils watered blue, brown, grey, green against their wills: wondering where they'd been.

When they broke the clasp, the world had forever changed. They'd almost suffocated in hollow dark, longing to catch an air.

They left him alone, Cellohead. He carried a cell on his back: released them every time he played.

The Leader

Orchestras were arenas of competition, he knew that. Second violins all harmony, not enough of the tune. Violas were failed fiddles, cellos too frequently plucked along.

Starting last desk, he was full of ambition: heads would topple one by one. He used his bow like a riding crop. In sectionals, he shone like flowers thrown.

He swayed to the tempo, led from the back. Till, at last, the front desk . . .

When his partner retired with nobbled hands, it was the culmination of his Masterplan.

Applause as he entered like a matador. His solos struck home like spears in hide. He bowed as the brass cowed behind.

Assured at the front, nowhere else to go, he eyed the virtuoso. It would never be him, raised on the concerto, spinning strings till they glow.

Close to the soloist, bow a pointing dagger now. Left hand shook with too much vibrato. The conductor glowered, lifting his baton-whip.

He was a slave in a galley. The others kept rhythm. He knew that orchestras were condemned ships.

Petrified Music

Two Stradivariuses under the bed in Monopoly Mayfair, where remarks were cut with diamonds.

Found concealed under the springs which held his final rest, the collector. Under his body which had turned to rotten wood, perfect specimens encased, unplayed for decades. The famous cellist discovered them. His own instrument had come to grow from him, marrying his form like no woman. His bow a third arm to wave adieu to the old man as ivy choked, as moss and lichen shrouded.

The famous cellist who never saw those violins, cellos, bows like his dear one. Saw them instead like paintings in some Royal Vault, buried and unseen.

The countless items the old man had amassed in safes, in lockers, stashed away in kidnap-coldness from the many players who could have courted their sounds, filled their hollowness.

In his flat, teabags hung drying, bare linoleum a blur of pattern, a single-barred fire reminded of wrapped blankets in the armchair. In his flat, the last crust still waited to be turned on its back.

All those petrified instruments released into daylight, like miners on a day trip. Strings so expectant for a touch that never came, eyes floating off to the horizon knowing they could drown in the current's force.

Sonatas, concertos, quartets, oratorios: scores like driftwood along the shore.

Crack

Stumbling and dodging swings of invisible truncheons: out into the midnight town comes Crack. The *boyz* have all pulled, while he plays with his can, long and hard. His eyes are helicopters, his nose-ring a runaway bull's.

He scrawls through the streets, grabbing the last inch of space on the roller blinds and below CCTV he sprays his spittle-sayings on grey metal – CRACK 4 EVER and KILL ALL PlGS. His *best but* Flash has gone down for trading: rotting inside like a growth they'd cut.

The Continental walkway's pink walls are too much of a temptation. All across their posh, clean faces he marks his messages of revenge and hate – PIGS ARE FILTH and CRACK DONE IT.

A girl, out of her skull, has draped herself across the pavement. Crack stops and raises his painty weapon – 'Yew wan' some?' She scream-laughs, kicking her legs. He daubs her with a cross: it's either treasure or target. She ups and lurches off – 'Oo-er, what a nutter!'

Uphill to home he's turning, turning back to the tedium of his real name.

Child of Dust

Cuddly bears, dogs and kangaroos. A hillock of toys all tied with inscriptions: *To Kayleigh, Babes, RIP*. One with a poem meticulously handwritten:

> *I never knew you,*
> *But for me*
> *Your loss will be*
> *As great as any sea*

A monument of colours: pink bears, blue dogs, but always true-brown kangaroos. There on the pavement, piled against the rust-scabbed gate, where the pockmarked road turns from estate to estate. There where the school javelin-fence runs out and ponies graze on nearby banks for bareback outlaws nobody argues with. There before the lawn's smeared mat. There where he returned that night after a *sesh* with the boys, brewed steep, but never enough to shut it out.

Never enough to stop his craving for the white moondust, melted to make the dark side light.

It was gone from his hiding-place, disintegrated into powdered skin. His deep crater eyes. She'd stolen his purpose. She was already asleep. Kayleigh cwtshed up, in his space. She snored like his old fella drunk from Bitter. Kayleigh kicked and rolled, always on the edge of crying out: meteor falling towards his head.

He had to . . . the dust would liquify in his veins, blood turn with the tide.

He shook her awake – 'Kar! Kar! Karen!' He tore off her mask, her oxygen. His voice a pointed pole down Kayleigh's throat. Her siren-wail was police chasing, was ambulance taking memories of his mam, was fire roasting his heart black.

'What ave yow done? Where . . . where is it?'

Fists landing like craft crashing down onto buildings. Her words were people panicking, fleeing. Kayleigh an animal whose terror clawed his eardrums. She launched into him, her body hard, metallic, shrieks flying sparks of friction.

The siren went on and on, fanging at his throat. She held it aloft, accusing. Wouldn't stop, it scrabbed his brain.

'She's yewers! Yewers an all! Do summin!'

He put it out, swung it round and round in a crazed orbit. Half-weapon, half-machine, his Black Hole eyes Karen was lost in.

She hugged the baby's scream, all that remained. But it soared from her, above the ceiling, into god-knows-what. He wanted to white it out. Let go the missile-animal, so silence would save him.

No point! The sirens rang through the estate, cutting the night in half. He fell to earth, grounded. Once his Kar half-mooned around, once his own crushed and crumbled child of dust.

It rained for days. She never went back. The house an empty, floating wreck. On one wall a screen held on that moment: shadowed figures of blood.

It rained for days: soft toys slumped with weight of it, stems broke like fragile skulls. Words ran away down cards and pages, merged like tributaries. Her name *Kayleigh* blotching and losing, finally losing its shape.

Barry Island Lines

'Got two hands and a ticking heart? Right, when can you start?'

On the lines, plates on the conveyor belt. *Factory don't wait for me* Beetheartery . . . in a passing touch, electricity. Finding your skin after hours of boredom.

Fingerprints on the boiled eggs, sweat in the gravy.

The day we went faster and faster, chanting like a war-dance, plates piled high in a jack-knife crash, food spilling its leathery guts. Till the manager sounded a gruff Glaswegian brake.

On the lines, tropically tired. Roast spuds like grenades and the cabbage vat stirred by a green-haired youth, one of Bowie's Martians. The Jackson-pushers with their steam connections, tanks full of hot dishes for ammunition.

'You're a fuckin student, tell me how this can be a fuckin island?'

Beach parties, police sirens, a pyre of deckchairs burning the days. Stoned on sand, waking in the arms of a ginger stranger. The girl on ganga wading into the sea fully-clothed, never wanting to return.

Come back, we will dance the ballroom with a blow-up doll. Come back, we will read Chekov as the tannoy announces: 'Security alert! Someone reading Russian Lit. by the fences!'

GOOD MORNING CAMPERS!

We are below Security, Red Coats and Blue. We are white hats soaked in B.O. We learn to pull dead animals apart, making them reasonable. We watch the frozen chickens thaw in cooler moments. We identify the fingerprints on food. Avoid them.

Promising Light

(for Al Jones, photographer)

'Omo!' and 'Daz!' they call him: mud-layered,
unwashed skin. Even here he can hear the children
taunting, fingers to ears at their low-flying brays.

Out of focus, in smokey mist, the skip slobbers a
piece of rag and a battlefield of rubbish reveals the
bones of all we consume.

He wears his medals proudly: keys dangled from
his lapel, the caravan his waiting shell. He'll crawl
into it like some wounded crustacean.

His hair reaches out: brown-grey bines the only
bush on a decimated moor. Fagin-featured, yet he'd
steal nothing, preferring to rummage among dead-
ends, where Third World meets First. Outcrop of his
wrinkled brow promising light the clouds deny.

Above Us, The Deed

Gathered in the car-park, bulldozer-made landscape, piles of rubble tied up with unfinished roads. Umbrella banners.

Footbridge over by-pass: major surgery, new organ. Into unexplored land for me, an old hand guides us. A tip still juts out, an awkward growth.

The sky's heavy as the path's mud. 'Merthyr's rainforest', I can believe it: birdfull, dripping, thunder beyond willows, birches, oaks. All the time from the hillside opposite a lung-sawing sound of diggers. King Coal – demented monarch – still in power despite planted communities of shrubs and saplings.

That noise stalks me. One moment in Belfast, scan the sky for an army chopper.

Historical detectives along the disused railway, a trail of stones, a rotting sleeper overgrown. Bridges span, sturdier than homes. FUCK U fading. Brunel's tunnel through the mountain, not listed, an industrial cavern.

Wide pond: we hear of a kingfisher, sign of clarity, returning. Yet a car rears up from water, rusted and mangled grin of 'So what?'

So what, it'll all be taken. So what, you walk. Walk for the last time. Under us, mineral. Above us, the deed.

The butterfly-man flits away chasing a rare breed. The bird-man points to a slit in a wall, nest he'd shown his grandchildren, fledglings opening beaks to receive.

Partly Political Conference

Someone has moved to suspend Standing Orders from the wall-bars! Whoever thought of a political conference in a leisure centre.

All remarks are addressed to two empty chairs and the Chair. The Chair has just informed us that the Tories were never socialist. Serious debate has begun.

Green-skinned people are being subjected to racist immigration laws. Poker-faced delegates amend the amendments, voting on whether we should vote.

'Uk!' goes the delegate from Newport, just west of London. 'Uk!' he does his seal impersonations, balancing the thesis and antithesis like a child prodigy gymnast.

The synchronized voting is the main feature of the afternoon. Unfortunately, the rival teams are quickly sinking. The count's impossible, as hands wave under the surface.

There is a great show of disunity. Any talk of confidence is premature.

The only party is a little girl's birthday in an adjoining room, where everyone gets a slice of the cake as it should be.

Strange Fish

They were hunched over fertility charts in a pub named *The Varsity*. Varsity? Surely that was Oxbridge not Aber: three decades from degrees in Snooker, American Studies subsidiary.

One admitted his sperm were addicted to Shiraz, so he'd bought four cats instead. He chatted with one for 5 minutes every evening.

Another had had a reverse vasectomy cock-up (literally). His sperm were deformed.

(They later saw a mural of these outside the Students' Union). He only had the one cat, compensation.

The third didn't care for charts. Met his partner in a siding north of Leeds. Their carriages were coupled, then went in opposite directions.

The last had hired himself out to political masters. His sperm-bank a sound investment. His wife suffered from felinophobia.

They'd all come a long way since the Revolution was round the corner, over the mountains, across the sea.

Joined together again by the net. Comparing the strange fish they'd caught.

Letter to Engels

My Liebe Friedrich,

I am, as ever, in your debt. That is not to say I share your guilt: the tarmacadam black as slave-ships, cotton white as the whipping hands.

Money is the base from which we build, of course. Without it the pillars of print would crumble, their leathery tiles fall and crack.

France is the building I would dismantle, only to restore again. The imprint of kings on its gold ware. Rise of the bourgeoisie from its parlours. No roof without foundations.

How you would laugh! Myself, English impostor Charles Marx, incarcerated in a hovel-cell for pawning Jennychen's silver! They saw this German refugee with long beard full of contradictions: a demon thief in some manor house looting the family Argyll.

Little Fawksey is the cunning one. He tricked a loaf from the claws of a predator. He has the guile of a Robespierre.

Jenny is large yet again. I fear for her health, her face the palest plaster, the babe a sagging in walls.

My enemies make much of my *faux pas*. They gang, like police spies in shop doorways, to vilify. I cannot reveal too much, my dear friend, as even pens have been known to confess. Suffice it that Jennychen has been thrown into a cellar of melancholy among rumour-rats.

I ask you, not for myself . . . The girls must learn that books will open secret doors and the piano be a vehicle for journeying (each score a nation).

Not for myself alone. I still keep Pieper, though he abuses my confidence. His study is a four-poster bed, his only sheets are ones he's soiled in bawdy pursuits.

Drink spares me daily torment, I regret. I am down in the dark with my Jenny, a fallen brandy-spider floating in the barrel. I do not hear the knocking of debtors, the bailiffs and rent collectors. I am Shakespeare's Porter after many more.

Around me, our furniture becomes bald, chairs lose their legs and damp is always besieging. Even the children's glee cannot decorate the jaded patterns.

In the Reading Room I strive to make order of it all. How servants feed and tend and without them, how would the Master survive? He'd be a helpless infant fumbling with buttons, this captain of crop or machine.

My good friend, you write so eloquently for me in the *Tribune*. You are surely my other half, my strategy, my eyes into the workings of the mill: its capacity to make mere hands from bodies, to take away the will. Conversely, to join: so many hands scarred or blackened by the selfsame lines.

I have been a fugitive too long. From this city, I can create theories higher and firmer of purpose: not the gardens of philosophy alone, but a world of words out of the past into the future, wherever that may belong.

Notes:
I am grateful to Francis Wheen's excellent biography of Karl Marx.
Little Fawksey – nickname of Marx's son
Jennychen – his wife, Jenny
Pieper – his secretary
Tribune – New York Tribune (newspaper)

Girl on the Viaduct

She perched herself there surprisingly comfortably, waiting for the night train, the ghost train.

When she was a teenager she'd never have considered it. Her recurrent dreams of falling. Constantly on look-out for her little bro' Bri (Bri for Bright she always said). Down, down . . . even though she could swim through air most times.

And now, it didn't matter.

The town had spat her out, rejected her. Where was her notoriety now? Front page, the *Cwm Gazette*. She'd made it. She had lost it.

This viaduct was nicknamed 'The Arches.' Her dad had bored her with stories about railways. She'd ignored him then. But now he was gone she heard his voice more clearly, enthusing about connections, junctions and decrying closures. Her mam, with that jolly Italian smile, teasing him.

'Trains, Daveed! The only trains you get here are ghost ones. Have you seen them, my Katie?'

Her Katie. Her mam up with the birds, a flight of geese going south to warmer climes. Her dad pacing along the missing line, sleeper to sleeper, but with nothing there.

Her sight swooped down to the little river, the Taf something. No dizziness, just a sense of power. All that was left. She dangled her legs onto the solid surface like a puppet. No god pulled her strings.

She faced away from town towards the Beacons, towards the winding river which cut deeper than its width would ever suggest. The flat plains of grassy banks resembled kept lawns, between rocky waters and steep slopes of thick woodland and bushes.

The town had expected so much. And then those songs . . . Chrissy, the guitarist had written them, but Katie knew they told the truth. They weren't what people wanted to hear. They were tales of pettiness and a people who wouldn't stand up, but turned upon each other to rob or grab what they could.

She hummed one of them, but it was the lyrics which burned inside. She wanted to forget them, every one, to drop them into the tumbling, gushing froths of the Devil's Punchbowl downstream from the viaduct.

'Ey! Yew orright?'

From the other end of The Arches' path a bulbous man called out.

Katie nodded and flapped her arms, as if ready to take off. He seemed alarmed by this and strode rapidly along the rubbly line.

'Don' worry love. I'll be there in a tick. Sorright!'

Katie thought he was about to yank her back into safety, so she acted quickly.

'I'm jest admirin the view. It's lovely up yer,' she tried to sound placid.

The toad-faced man with large black-rimmed specs leant near her strategically.

'Thought yew woz abseilin or summin . . . The

160

missis seen yew. I'm the lan'lord up there, see. No abseilin allowed yer now. Not since . . . it's the rools.'

'Na, I'm jest waitin. Sooner or later my train'll turn up.'

He frowned at her, suspecting madness. What to do next?

'Look love, it's too risky. Yew get all kinda nutters up by yer. Boyz on booze 'n' drugs, all sorts . . . 'ey could take advantage . . . why don' yew come up my pub an I'll buy yew a nice drink. There's an even better view from-a beer garden.'

'Are yew tha desprut f' customers? . . . Look, yew're very kind an 'a, but I don' need no Samaritans. No way I'm gunna jump.'

The landlord weighed her up. Attractive girl: deep, dark eyes. Too pale and tatty though. Didn't eat properly. Standard denims, but attitude nose-rings. He couldn't work her out. Something hidden.

'Yew shewer? My missis ull . . .'

'Onest. There's no problem. I'm on'y sittin.'

He shook his head, unsure. Peered to the top of the slope for a semaphore message from his wife. Reluctantly, he turned and waddled away, leaving Katie to herself again.

STREET PULSE: it wasn't even that good a name. But then the Stereophonics was naff and what about Catatonia, a state of paralysis for goodness' sake? Next to the 60 Foot Dolls, Street Pulse was positvely poetry. And Chrissy had been there from the start. Her other half until . . .

There were people below waving up to her: three

lads with lager cans hooked to their paws, like the landlord's fear made human. You couldn't escape it. Chrissy had said it right in 'Weapons of Glass' . . .

Where alcohol is the fuel
And love is up the arse –
Saturday nights with weapons of glass . . .

There she was yet again. Going back, when she wanted to go down. Down into flight, not drowning or the final crack.

One of the boys took out his plonker and pissed. He shook it while the others gestured at her and pointed at his barely-visible penis.

'Ey love!' he yelled, 'do us a favour, jump an land on me will ya?'

Katie shuddered her legs wide and instantly regretted it. They weren't an audience, just three pathetic lads out to taunt. They reacted with typical excitement, wooahing and corring, while Katie tried to send them up with a snigger they'd hardly detect.

Another man ambled along the viaduct, accompanied by a woman. They didn't talk. The man was dressed casually, while the woman looked too chic for a country jaunt. As they approached Katie, he stared deliberately at her. As they passed, his eyes followed her, his wife tutting at this all-too-customary behaviour. He stopped abruptly, like a train at fallen boulders.

'C'mon Mart, yew promised me a tidee drink after all this walkin.'

He continued to eye Katie.

'Bloody ell, Mart, yew never give over d' yew?'

'Wise up, Lou, she's an ex pupil.'

162

At the familiar 'wise up', Katie returned his full focus for the first time. His wife, hands on hips, daring him to be over zealous.

'Sir . . . I . . . Ow's thin's?'

She sounded so relaxed given the fact that she was balanced on a viaduct hundreds of feet above the narrow valley floor.

'Mart! Yew comin or wha?'

Katie's former Geog. teacher tried to contain his annoyance.

'Louise, yew go ahead. I'll catch up. I won't be long.'

His wife shrugged acceptance and plodded off, muttering disgust. While Martin leaned close to Katie, examining her eyes for a response.

'Katie, I aven't seen yew for ages. Not since all the . . .'

'I know . . .'

'I thought yew'd made it Bigtime . . . Oh God! Yew . . . I mean . . .'

He suddenly contemplated the drop.

'Yew wern thinkin of . . . What appened, Katie? Tell me.'

He moved even closer now. She knew he was ready to grip.

She laughed at his concern. He was shocked.

'Yew know, sir . . . I mean, Mr Davies . . . yew always woz my eero, y'know. Ever since yew took us on tha field trip an bought us all them drinks.'

He'd been a sucker. They'd led him on. He got into trouble when the parents found out. Been given a warning.

'Really? I thought . . . yew know . . . I thought the kids always took the piss outa me.'

He'd dropped his pen on the floor deliberately to ogle at girls' legs. 'Pervy Marty' they'd dubbed him. But Katie was pleased with any audience now, even him. He was uncomfortably near, his breath against her neck, puffing.

'The train'll come eventually, Mr Davies. My dad promised it would.'

Martin Davies was thrown by her sudden distracted talk. He wondered if she'd had a breakdown and this really was a suicide attempt.

'What happened to the band, Katie? Yew were doin great. I remember goin to that gig in the Kooler Club an . . .'

Katie's mood altered again. She reluctantly spat her memories out.

'Yeah, it all changed. Ev'rythin! Chrissy wrote all them songs . . . they tol the truth . . . nobody wanted t' yer it . . . I got my own manager, tried t' go solo. I woz so fuckin crap Mar . . . Mr Davies. Without Chrissy I wuz nothin . . . Thought I could be Cerys Catatonia . . . Katie Cwmtaff, eh? All attitude an no fuckin talent whatsoever.'

Martin was scared. This girl now seemed on the edge. He was ready to pounce, to catch her. She stared longingly into the emptiness in front of her. He tried to twist his neck towards her and touched her arm doing so. Excited by her cold flesh. She recoiled: a sudden flashback of grovelling on the classroom floor.

'My mam woz a bird Mr Davies. I wish I could

164

join er . . . But my dad . . . maybe ee'll be drivin tha train when it comes.'

'Katie, don't get yewrself all worked up . . . if I really woz yewr hero, lissen t' me now. Jest come off there an come with me for a drink or somethin. Meet my wife, then after that we cun jump together . . . I mean . . .'

'Sir . . . yew wozn my eero, yew woz a right plonker! Now leave me be, will yew?'

Martin backed off, baffled by her wayward nature.

'I . . . er . . .'

'Jest piss off, right? . . . I int gunna jump! . . . Don' feel guilty. Go f'r a pint. Forget it!'

Her eyes were still lusciously exotic despite the haggard features and neglected hair. A swift sense of her legs, under the desk, long and lovely, leading . . . The girl was obviously deranged. He moved further away.

'Alright! I know when I'm not wanted.'

'Too true.'

He headed for the pub and a tongue-lashing. How far down could you go, he thought. Katie had been up there. Cool Cymru, wasn't it? After the Manics so much expected. He liked their stuff . . . Street Pulse. He'd only seen them once. At the very back, leaning against the bar, posing as an A & R man.

Below her, those boys had disappeared. It was gradually darkening. Annoyingly, one of Chrissy's songs revolved in her head:

Dark days of boarded-up brains
Of tunnels, tablets, graffiti stains . . .

Bleak words, but they matched her mood. She was

165

glad Davies had gone. Creep. Touchy, crawly. The small valley peaceful again. When darkness came . . . Shouts from the other side of the viaduct. The three boys cavorting towards her, two swinging sticks, the other calling out.

'Ey, yew gunna jump, or wha? Takin yewer time, in yew?'

The stick-swingers guffawed. She actually thought of moving on, but couldn't. There was nowhere to go.

In a moment they were around her, a dog-pack sniffing. She tilted her body from one side to the other as they beat the wall with their sticks behind her. They were all glassy-eyed, not plate-glass but jagged and knife-like. Each one goaded.

'Yer! Woz tha yewer fancy-man or wha?'

'Yew bin screwin im?'

'Spread yewr legs agen, eh? Like yew done from below!'

Katie stood up on the parapet facing them. A hostile audience. A Club where all they wanted was Heavy Metal covers.

'See them sticks, well suck on them! Coz tha's all yew boyz 've got.'

It wasn't a clever put-down, but the gall was enough.

'Aw, fuck off yew loony-toon!'

They threw their sticks at her and she wobbled, surprising herself by flapping her arms, as though she'd grown feathers. The leader of the pack jeered.

'C'mon boyz, le's leg it. She's mental.'

They ran off down the path, still mocking – 'Loony toon! Loony toon!'

Katie resumed her former posture. Let the light go down with her future. She felt weak and hollow-headed. She fancied she could hear a train in the distance, but it could easily have been a plane overhead.

Then, out of the welcome silence of the line, out of its long throat fading into the tunnel of trees, came her father's voice, informing, declaiming: 'See Katie, love. Wales woz once the centre of steam. We done it first an now . . . look at this . . . nothing! On'y a bare track t' walk an fill with memrees.'

With his final words an explosion of birds, of starlings rising from bushes and trees clattering wings as though her mam's tongue was chiding him for being too depressing.

Katie felt she could remain here, poised on stone. Caught between the ghost-voices of those that mattered most, with no crowd below, in the darkness, waiting for her to drop.

Scott Guru

When it all began it's hard to tell. A series of coincidences maybe. Or confluences would be a better word. And a word was, after all, the spark.

In any case, here I sit in the Head's office, not being offered a doughnut to ease my suffering, or the possibility of promotion should I regularly attend the Advanced Learning Strategies Committee, whatever that might be.

No, I feel as if I've molested a pupil. Exposed myself to a group of Year 7 girls. Accessed porn on the internet when doing NOFF training (which earned me a free computer bag full of bumf, but no laptop). He is staring more severely than ever before. Not since my class were accused of bouncing on the computer chairs by regular informant, the Computer Technician. Not since I was accused of truancy after taking two days off following the 'Staff Do.' (Okay, I was hungover, but that didn't explain the food poisoning).

He is generally a genial man, but prone to believing unreliable tales. This time I could hardly protest my innocence as his words float over my head and up to the trophy cabinet. My deeds had tarnished the school's reputation. How could I? A young boy!

168

It all seems about someone else. This evil man who had pursued the pupil so rigorously. A matter for the Governors, he says. I doubt if you'll ever. After 30 years!

A mid-life crisis or what?

Yes, I think it may have begun with the course on Stress Management. I wanted to be sitting near to Suzie Edwards. Young, long dark hair, shapely-bummed if rather horsey-toothed when laughing. But that smile. My wife used to give me smiles like that once. Before the Ice Age. Must be a fantasy. Maybe for anyone. I wanted to sit next to her. All I got was Ken Mullen, Geog. teacher. No way, both of us scowled, were we going to perform acupressure on each other. The Stress Management course just increased my stress. Made me a lot less able to manage it.

I merely felt isolated, as all the rest joined in with the exercises at the bidding of the Doctor/Expert. I felt totally frustrated as I watched youthful and tall Sports teacher Mark Watkins manipulate Suzie and could hear her giggling rise larkish in a hall full of tittering.

Try it out breaktime. Find a willing colleague. Only takes a matter of minutes.

And then, the breathing. That served to increase my heartbeat instead of the desired relaxation. Choose an image or word to exhale. Breathe in. Breathe out: Suzie's bum.

The photocopy machine. From behind. My alltime favourite position. Thump, thump, thump . . . My heart boxed in, trying to be let out.

That night I woke up at 3am. Unaccountably

169

sweating in mid-winter. It wasn't the impending Inspection either, which whirled ceaselessly in my head like bats in a dome. It was the fact that I had all the symptoms of a stressed teacher. Till the Doctor said, I'd never noticed them before.

My headache was nothing to do with the double nightcap I'd slugged back. My backache related in no form to a wrestling match with our delinquent wheelie-bin. My night-sweats definitely not a feature of the male menopause. My inability to get back to sleep nothing whatsoever to do with sex deprivation.

No, I was a walking advert for the syndrome the Doc. had described that day.

'Why are you up?' my wife sleep-slurringly enquired. A short enough phrase which actually meant – 'How dare you wake me up in the middle of the night with your petty problems just because you're a teacher you seem to think you have a special right to anxiety . . . well, let me tell you Council employees with bosses on their backs have their own problems which you can't hope to appreciate can you?'

That day I went to work dosed with pain-killers, feeling like I should've gone bunking down the shops with the worst of the Year 10-ers. The pills couldn't numb the faces of certain pupils, which nagged like my wife wanting something fixed. The jeering, sneering features of Rhys Carnott and John Lewis-Smith. In particular. Carnott, a gob and fart machine, swinging on his chair and constantly chewing. Lewis-Smith, who could make a paper plane for Wales but was allergic to writing: an ADS victim who had become immune to Ritulin.

I didn't know my time-table. I didn't want to. That way I had nothing to dread, except when it arrived in my room.

So Year 7 first off was a relief: still in awe of the sheer size of the place and even enthusiastic, would you believe? A lesson without lateness, boredom and underhand listening devices. They actually paid attention when I asked 'What are paragraphs? . . . Are they, for example, parrots keen on Maths?' A few complimentary laughing-moans.

When they were busy later on – planning accounts on topics of interest – I squatted next to Scott Bircham, a ruddy-faced boy who either found everything impossible or couldn't be bothered. At my posture, Carnott would've done chicken impressions and Lewis-Smith gone 'Perwaw!' to indicate my halitosis.

'Why aren't you writing anything, Scott?'

'It's my knuckle, sir. I smashed it on the garden wall this morning.'

'How did you do that?'

'Only joking, sir. Ah-ha!'

At which, he drew out his perfectly white knuckle from under the table.

'Right! You're planning your paragraphs . . . What's your topic? Sport?'

'Yeah!'

'Right! What sports do you like?'

'Rugby football snooker motorbikes kickboxing cricket.' All in one breath.

'Right! Write a paragraph on each one and at the end say what you'd like to do in the future. What would you like to do, Scott?'

'Landerim!'

'Eh?'

Others at the table joined in, amused at my bewilderment. They knew Scott, I didn't.

'He means lavender, sir. But that's a flower isn't it?'

'He's mad, sir!'

'Lavender, Scott? You want to be a flower?'

'No, landerim. That's it. I've heard of it anyway.'

'Did you just make that up, Scott? Like your knuckle.'

He mused at me pleasantly, yet blankly. Wherever this 'landerim' had come from, there were certainly no clues on his face.

The Head sits upright, as if to deliver a verdict.

'Invented, Chrisssssss!' he still maintains the familiarity, though the sibilance gives away his true intent. 'Before I get the Authority involved . . . give you an opportunity . . . you're saying this . . . only in Year 7 for goodness' sake! . . . what in God's name possessed you? . . . Well?'

He peers hard, wanting to find concrete evidence of some mid-life crisis which had brought on this weird behaviour.

That evening after Scott had uttered 'landerim', his face stayed with me, but not with the menace of Carnott or Lewis-Smith. I recalled Jenny Mumford, who'd become so obsessed with one recalcitrant delinquent that she began to hallucinate him into every single lesson she taught. He'd be there sitting, smirking at her. She began to leave classrooms as

172

soon as she 'saw' him. One day she left a classroom, only to find him outside the room as well, hanging about, smoking in open defiance. He blew smoke straight into her face and she never returned.

But this was different. Scott was like some benign Buddha-figure, whose strange word captivated me.

It was that very evening that I escaped my wife's appalling taste in TV programmes: The Bill, Casualty, Holby City . . . just about anything where young, glamorous doctors or coppers had loads of time for affairs in wards or police-cars and still saved lives or caught criminals in their spare time. I put on Robert Wyatt. Music I've followed devoutly from way back, from Soft Machine to Matching Mole. Late teens. An Intellectual with a capital P (for Prat). 'The Moon in June.' . . . was that an electric shaver in the background? A brandnew CD of 'Rock Bottom' to replace my old and battered vinyl. Then I heard it for the first time: first track, second side, even though it was one-sided. He sang it. I checked the word. Yes, it was there on the song. Unmistakable. 'Landerim.' Just as Scott.

From then on, Scott's powers were obvious. He was operating on the same level as my all-time hero, the remarkably unique Robert Wyatt. He could tell me other things if only I tapped into his thoughts.

The next day I kept him behind after the lesson.

'Sir, I didn't mean it!'

'Mean what, Scott?'

'I was only making a chain out of paperclips. I didn't know they were yours.'

I hadn't even noticed. I had been too busy giving

them nonsense poems to write in the hope that more connections would emerge.

'Oh, don't worry . . . paperclips, you say?'

A garland fit for him. I would make one. Adorn him.

'No, no . . . I just need to check your work.'

I fingered through his tatty excercise-book, found the word, checked the spelling. Searched for his poem.

'Where's your poem, Scott?'

'There, sir!'

He pointed to a torn part of the latest page. His face took on a cartoon grin.

'But . . . there's nothing there, Scott.'

'Well . . . '

'Yes?'

'I chewed it up! Sorry sir! It didn't make no sense.'

For a moment I forgot who he was.

'You what?'

'Sorry, sir!'

'It wasn't supposed to make any sense. That was the point. What about your 'Landerim', that didn't make sense either.'

'That's what I wanna be though.'

'A landerim?'

'Yeah.'

I examined his face: so sincere, so plausible.

'Ever heard of Rob Wyatt, Scott?'

'Rugby player, ain't he?'

A landerim, Scott. So you shall be.

'To be perfectly honest, Chrissssss . . . stress problems, don't you think? . . . You should consider seeing a doctor. That bracelet, for goodness' sake, what were you thinking of?'

'No doughnuts then?'

'Chrissss . . . are you listening?'

'Chris, are you listening to me? I think you've got minute headphones on all the time . . . I'm going out tonight, alright? With the girls from the department. Bit of a celebration. Julie's got engaged.'

'That's fine. We'll be alright together, me and Rob.'

'Who's Rob?'

'Wyatt . . . who else?'

'How can you listen to that stuff, it's not normal . . . it's just . . . weird!'

When she eventually returned, singing like an upside-down jukebox and clattering into everything, I was listening to 'Solar Flares Burn For You', admittedly erratic and obscure. I had finished the garland and was sipping red. She hovered over, a drunken buzzard ready to pounce.

'We had a great time, Chris . . . brilliant laugh . . . What is that?'

'Robert Wyatt . . . I told you . . . '

'No, that!'

She grabbed my paperclip craftwork and shook it. I thought it would scatter across the room.

'Have you been making me some jewellery, Chris? Oh, how sweet of you! I'll wear it for you, shall I? . . . And switch that bloody crap off, it's doing my head in!'

I obliged without argument, knowing her mood could change by the second when drunk.

'Give it back! It's for my Year 7 class tomorrow. You'll break it.'

'Ooo,ooo . . . tetchy tetchy tetchy, aren't we?'

She dance-swayed around, twirling the garland which amazingly held firm, then threw it onto my lap.

'Well, anyway, we met these real hunks. They were gorgeous. I bet they hadn't even heard of Robert Wyatt.'

'So that's a sign of taste, is it?'

'Yes, Chris, as far as I'm concerned, it is.'

That night as she snored in time with the central-heating system, I couldn't sleep. My head was a whirligig of paperclips and landerims, of blank pages of exercise books with bits chewed off. Homage. Communion. Worship. Not even fantasies of Suzie could blank out my single-mindedness.

Next day in the photocopy room, she was leaning over the machine when I entered. On her line of bare back between jumper and hip-huggers I saw a tattoo for the first time. It was a colourful Celtic design, curvy and snakey.

'Oh, it's you!' she turned and caught me a quick glance.

'Sorry, I'll come back later.'

Until it was time for Year 7's, I rehearsed in my head what should have been.

'You like Celtic designs, then?'

'Oh, I see what you mean. Yes, very original.'

'Yeah, it's something to aim for.'

Once settled, they were ready for the ceremony. The revelation of Scott Guru.

176

'Okay! Right! Listen! Shshshshshshsh! . . . As you know, you were doing nonsense poems last lesson. Well, Scott here has made up a strange word "Landerim" . . . '

'It's not . . . '

'Okay, Scott . . . well, he wants to be a landerim and that's exactly what he shall be . . . this lesson!'

Giggling, groaning, guffawing.

'Sir, I ain't . . .'

'Right, Scott. You come up here and sit on my desk.'

He reluctantly shambled to the front. I placed the garland of paperclips over his head.

'I ain't wearing no necklace!'

'Scott, you were making one of these yesterday with my paperclips.'

He was beginning to see the whole process as a humiliating punishment, rather than a religious rite of deep significance.

'Sir, I'm sorry. Now let me sit down.'

'No, Scott. This is important. You are the landerim and the class must pay their respects . . . Right, everyone! Tear part of a blank page from your excercise books, chew it up and then make a line in front of Scott.'

I instructed every member of the class to pile up their chewed paper in front of Scott as offerings. Some of the others wanted to be the landerim after that and Scott felt quite proud.

'I still think he meant lavender, sir!' quipped Josh.

'And then, there's the matter of the rat, Chrisss.'

'Ah yes, that came after.'

'Why, Chris, why?'

'It's hard to explain. The boy Scott, he mentioned the Chinese Year of the Rat and then spotted a rat in the Quad. It all fitted together somehow.'

'But to bring a dead rat into the classroom and to get all the class to dance around it chanting?'

He leans forward, ready to pronounce judgement. I have undoubtedly sinned. All his amiability turns to sternness.

'Look, I'm sorry, Chris, but this has gone far enough. We've had numerous complaints from parents. I've defended you for far too long. Why don't you become a priest? You seem that way inclined.'

'There's only one thing I don't understand.'

'What's that, Chris?'

'How Scott managed to draw that Celtic design in his book.'

He rose now to usher me out. A hopeless case.

'Chris, Chrissss. Take a break. Look for another purpose in life.'

He was back to chummy now, my future decided. He still didn't offer a doughnut. That was it. Thirty years in education ended because of a guru child, a beatific boy adorned in paperclips who, with only Robert Wyatt and myself, shared the secret of that single enigmatic word, 'landerim.'

No Ordinary House

It began with a house, as it so often does. But this was no ordinary house. Its roof of grass for one thing. Its white boney frame another. And the well at its centre. The cellar you could only open at night. Attic with its nursery chimes.

I had lived there alone too long. The well had become everything. Down its depths I plunged my drawings: rough sketches, doodles, charcoal shadings. An artist of the void. I would watch captivated as my intricately-folded offerings disappeared. They were mortal just as I. They were pointless just as I. Eventually I'd join them. But not yet. Not just yet.

The others had left, tired of my terse tediousness. I have forgotten their names. Once I was a man of the times: I would proclaim, protest. Now I have no contact except the reports, the evidence of next-door.

This property is of some value, I'd say. Though the roof has grown too long and the frames are rickety, what house could boast such a well and water too, where my papers float and mingle, smudge the surface.

This property has no value to me whatsoever, except that I long again to venture down its cellar, to climb up to its attic and play in a treasure trove of trinkets and objects each with a memory stored in their spin, their repetitive tunes, their clockwork voices.

Then one day it all changed forever. A stranger at the door. I wondered whether to answer. In the narrow ajar, he spoke from inside his long leather coat. A gun, protruding from its neck like a menacing snake, forced me to listen.

'You'll take me in!'

'Will I?'

'That's what they said.'

'Did they?'

'You're on the list.'

'I can't be.'

'You are. This is a safe house. They're after me. You must.'

I let him in. There was only a single chair. He sat in it. He filled the whole room with his troubles. I had no TV. I had no idea. I must hide the gun.

'You could throw it down the well.'

'Are you stupid?'

'They'd never find it.'

'Neither would I.'

'Or the cellar?'

'The cellar? Sounds promising . . . how do you get down there?'

'Go to sleep. Dream dangerously. I can't anymore.'

'That's a grand idea . . . Is there a bed?'

'Only one. You're welcome. I'll sleep in the chair.'

'If they come . . .'

'They?'

'You know, the enemies.'

'I don't know. I'm past . . .'

'You know what to do.'

'Do I?'

'Yes, you're on the list, remember?'

I showed him the double bed and its springs creaked and strained as he lay down, boots still on. He lay hugging the gun like a partner in crime, its barrel a straight spine.

'Look out the window, see if there's any signs,' he instructed.

There were two windows rather than the usual one. The right was cataracted by a soiled blind, never lifted. The other was my spy to their goings-on. I had noted the strangers in suits who came and went carrying equipment for monitoring.

There was nothing in the street save parked cars and a solitary caravan. Overhead I could hear a police helicopter in the distance, but that was common enough.

'Nothing! It's fine. Sleep well.'

'If the gun goes . . .'

'With another dream you'll get it back. It'll be safe down there.'

I left him there, snuggled next to his companion.

I tried to doze in the armchair after filling the mouth of the Aga with broken arms and legs of the furniture. Its glow was narcotic, but I was still perturbed by this stranger.

I could steal upstairs and snatch his gun. Throw it down the well. Hear the explosion of water echoing back. A long throat swallowing the problem whole like snake with egg.

The Aga stove devoured the contents of the house.

Soon there would be nothing left. Would that be the time for me to join my artwork? I would not know till it arrived.

I resolved not to take the gun. Whatever I'd signed up to, whatever I'd joined or done could not so easily be denied. It would be a betrayal.

I hoped he wouldn't wake early and discover my reports in the back room. They were detailed and accurate. They traced the noises next-door: the arguments, the way there was a voluminous snoring which shook the walls. They noted examples of odours which crept through paint and mortar. Above all, they commented on the machines I'd heard: the grumbling, rumbling, growling, prowling apparatus of spying I knew existed.

The man upstairs would surely laugh at my meticulous monomania. But he didn't know who my enemies were. Only his own, outside, in a world I couldn't share.

The more I contemplated him, the more my mind was lulled. Birds picked and beaked at his head, not mine. Blackbirds pulled at his roots, jackdaws skraked across the surface and crows dug deep for grubs. The Aga yawned smokily and I sank slowly, gradually below the floorboards.

I was there. I knew I was, because the walls glistened with tears. The cobwebs formed nets which veiled my face, as I descended the stone steps. Standing in the centre of the space of damp yet sparkling slabs was an old man. He held a tennis racket as if to hit me with it. He smiled recognition.

'It's about time!' he cracked, showing one brown tooth in his pinched mouth.

Only then did I realise I was carrying the gun, draped awkwardly over one shoulder.

'I'm sorry, it's just that . . .'

'No need. I understand. We all need a father. And yours? . . . well . . . The horse in the garden which bolted and hauled him along the road. The dog in the garage which chewed his riding-boots so he had it put down. And the car. Always the car as a weapon, when he drove in a mad rage. The car like the cockpit of a plane speeding straight for a cliffside'

'Yes, of course you're right. It is possible after all.'

I wanted to embrace his thin paleness, but years without touch thwarted me. Instead, I laid the gun down at his feet like an offering to a god. He passed me the racket in exchange.

'A fair trade, I'd say. It'll be safe here, don't worry . . . Do you play?'

'I think . . . I used to . . . I used to do a lot . . .'

'I'm glad you came. I knew you would.'

I swung the racket as if to please him. He picked up the gun and held it warily. He paced backwards into the rows of barrels, each labelled with a white, painted abbreviation.

I clutched the racket close to me. There were no goodbyes.

I awoke to the heaviness of a father found and a father lost. I rushed to the rim of the well in despair.

'Where? Where?' my shouts ricocheted off the sides and plummeted. The only reply from myself.

I turned to find the man pinning me against the brickwork. Now he had no gun he was all aggression. His face twitched and eyes drilled pneumatic. I quaked at their forcefulness.

'Where is it?'

'I told you.'

'But I never dreamt, did I? How . . . ?'

'I did it. It was the first time for ages. You'll get it back, no problem.'

'It's gone, isn't it? You stole it as I slept? You've thrown it down there, haven't you?'

He lifted me up and sat me on the edge. Behind was the threat of the final drop.

'You're working for them, aren't you? The list must've been . . .'

'No! Years ago I did take part. I marched . . . Listen! They're bound to come. I can help. You can live in the attic. They won't look there.'

'Why not?'

'It's perfectly disguised. Looks like another part of the ceiling. You step up and you disapppear. Easy as that.'

He let me go. I slid to the floor, sighing relief.

'Look what I got for your gun.'

On the chair the racket sat, propped up: its taut head, its single body-stem.

In one movement he grabbed it, swung himself around and, laughing ferociously, hurled it down the well. It made a clattering sound, like old teeth chattering and then was swallowed whole by a murky mouth.

'It was a gift.'

'Too bad, old son.'

The phone rang. Again he glared, commanding without a word . . . It was under a small table in the corner, which I'd spared so far.

I answered it: 'Hello? Hello? Who is it?'

I heard breathing, a whistle of nostrils. It was my father. He never said a word. He was the only one who called me now.

'Who?'

'I don't know. They didn't say anything.'

Now he closed in again. His body smelt of a stagnant pond. His stubble a field to be burnt.

'Are you not letting on?'

His breath rank as spread manure.

'No, honestly! . . . But if they are after you, why not go up there. You'll be totally safe.'

He was impressed by the camouflage. Each padded rectangle identical. Each like the cover of some large photo album.

'What the hell are all these papers? Why have you got a recording-machine?'

'It's nothing! Just my work.'

He became far too inquisitive: lifted a disk, slotted it in, pressed 'play'. Out came muffled sounds of tapping and then distinctive orgasmic moans: pleasure in the guise of pain. I hadn't even noticed them before, too intent on counting the beats of the tapping.

'You pervert!'

'I'm not. It's next door! They . . .'

The door-bell rang like a fire-alarm. He jumped to attention. He had no choice now.

185

'That one there! Third along from the window.'

Little did he know, each one a different entrance, a different time.

I squatted and he scrambled onto my shoulders. For a tall man he wasn't that weighty.

'How do I open it?'

'There's a clasp like a car-bonnet. Slide your hand underneath. Release it.'

'There's nothing here!'

The bell rang once more. Shrill panic.

I thought of the cot, the crib, the rocking-horse: how they would never be sacrificed to the fire . . . and the attic hatch sprung open, flapping downwards like an astounded expression.

He could discern only a black hole, like the very bottom of the well itself. He wrenched himself into it.

'I can't see a . . .'

'I'll get you a torch later.'

As soon as his feet disappeared, I slammed the hatch-door shut. He had fallen upwards. I imagined the long coat hanging from a mobile: still life.

The bell rang again. Persistent and annoying.

I peer-strained through the letter-box.

'Yes, who is it?'

No uniforms, just the belted belly of the man next-door. I recognized that midriff anywhere.

'Open up! We've had enough! . . . last night, all that rummaging around in the middle of the night. We don't even know where the bloody noises are coming from!'

'Go away! It won't do any good. I've got it all recorded. I know everything.'

'Everything? You're mad! . . . Anyway, we've seen the Department. It's all in here.'

An official letter struck me in the face and landed on the brushy mat below. With utmost disdain I immediately brought it to the well.

I must sketch again. I must try to catch the smile of that single-toothed elfin man who called himself my father. To show how his tears of longing dewed the cellar walls.

I scrumpled the Departmental letter into a projectile. I threw it and my laughter followed down, a buzzard chasing a sparrow.

The phone rang yet again. On the other end, I could hear a snuffle and throat-clearing, as if he was preparing to spit. My father was improving his communication skills. I snorted back, using his own language.

They would come soon, but I had consigned the stranger to a mere photo: a leather-coated gangle, hanging bat-like in the attic.

Houses are Marching

The houses are marching up our Valley. The main road is their artillery.

'Dereliction! Dereliction!' drear the officials, figures in columns, ignorant battalions.

Plug the shafts, pour concrete into galleries, build them on rafts. Oak trees will be felled like refugees.

Horses and cows on reed-wiry moors, sheep on higher pastures below the paraded conifers: all will be evacuated.

Underfoot, the gorse, heather, bracken and countless wild flowers will suffer scorched earth. Only *Llysiau Taliesin* will be saved, sealed and sent to Botanical Gardens.

Brunel's tunnel and Cwmglo Chapel pounded into rubble by diggers. Our past to be miniatured, plaqued, muralled.

Streams will be forced underground. They'll have to undermine executive estates in their own fashion. Ruled by culverts, water will be told to obey orders.

Frogs and newts, jays and larks, golfers and kissing couples, dog-walkers and boomerang throwers, rope-swingers and buzzards: the list nobody listens to, the numbers never quoted as statistics.

All the worth of the Waun dismissed by a mockery of street-signs.

Barnardo's Boy

I'm a Barnardo's Boy, pebbly beans and mushy pie.

I'm a Barnardo's Boy, day care project managing my temper trip orphan.

Orphan with a dad I don't know and my mental mam, my *off*-it mam taking the white tabs, eyes on the moon.

A Barnardo's Boy driven and dumped, slumping back waiting for the next adult to substitute. They come and go in rooms, these parents I adopt. Their names scraped out with shells in the sand. Their voices the sea at Porthcawl, Barry: the promise but the freezing reality.

In the soft room, in the padded play room, I try to build a bridge, a den. Knocked down I lose it totally, my head so hot with blood it's a balloon of sun. I become my disappeared dad, my mam's boss-booted friends, throwing the shapes at the wall, at anything that's moving. I want to kill the memories behind the paintwork.

I'm a Barnardo's Boy, but today I went on a long journey. I drew and wrote it out: my boat to the centre of the earth, where I was a magician and the dragon's fire lit my head. I steered through a flaming lake and it never burnt.

Duel in the snow

It was a duel in the snow. Incongruous, the rolling, factoried fields of East Anglia, of barley and sugar-beet and combine-harvesters, now plains of white.

We printed the lanes, trespassing across land owned by some huge pudding company. So far from homeland Cymru as chalk and Caerffili.

It was a duel in the snow at four paces apart. My sister and mother intoning Dylan, miners of that crackling black seam he sang way back below a mountain.

'As I was young and easy under the apple boughs' they boomed, voices fading westerly. No fruit from the solitary trees.

'Ah, you should see Cynddylan on a tractor . . .' I harked back, RS sharp, the machines waiting in their barns, ghosts of another season.

It was a duel in the snow. Nobody won. Our words fell, cloud-bursts from an exiled sea.

Just Like Kerouac

Looking back we wore the book. Its brown and white torn cover our jackets. Its firm spine the route the direct line we followed. Carlisle station our Denver, Ayr town our west our edge of it all.

I had thought somehow we'd failed Jack Kerouac, absurd thumb-prodders on the northbound motorway plodding the hard-shoulder illegally never picking a lift, finding that mountain on the map, heading for its YHA never realising the thousand feet above.

I'd thought we were two errant disciples, our bus more terrier panting up hills. Till, I wore it again, this time a multi-coloured coat, a photo montage of car to climbing clouds. And wearing it I knew it fitted now as ever before.

We had retraced his naive route to Great Bear Mountain, had witnessed the pugilism of Central City bars in Ayr taverns, felt the frozen loneliness of solitary hobos on that river-bank, our twig-formed fire outed by a forestry-worker. And that moment, that vision: a beebop zen revelation of trout leaping for flies at dawn, diving into air and drawing their shapes there.

Just like Kerouac we followed with eyes alone the many passing girls, roads with dead-end signs, never further than their names.

Except we pursued no Dean Moriarty. Our mutual friend, the black flag motorcycle Nietszchean with Kamikaze disguise was back in hometown Manchester as we stuttered west through Lockerbie, through 'Burns country' travelling always down into layers of history or gazing up to peaks we'd never attain.

The compass-points of his search the wheels that spun fast and away.